THE MYSTERIOUS SECRET OF FRANKLY WOODS

KATHLEEN W. FRANKS

A.H. STOCKWELL
PUBLISHERS SINCE 1898

Published in 2023 by
Kathleen W. Franks in association with
Arthur H Stockwell Ltd
West Wing Studios
Unit 166, The Mall
Luton, Bedfordshire
ahstockwell.co.uk

All characters appearing in this work are
fictitious. Any resemblance to real persons,
living or dead, is purely coincidental.

Contents

To my mum and dad for their unwavering love and support.

Also

Theresa, Jill, Matthew, Sunny and Magee.

THE MYSTERIOUS SECRET OF FRANKLY WOODS

Prologue

21ˢᵗ December 1943, England

It was a cold, clear winter night; stars twinkled brightly in the sky above.

The trees below bore white sleeves like strange, ghostly figures frozen to the spot in the icy landscape. It was the kind of night – for anyone with an ounce of sense – to stay indoors beside a roaring fire, though some did not take heed...

A young girl walked through the woods with her companion, her feet crunching on the crisp snow underfoot. Strangely, she did not feel the biting cold that whipped around her on the bitter breeze.

They reached a wooded glade. Young eyes grew wide at the sight that greeted them...

"Welcome to the midwinter festival, Anna!" Her companion, who was only a few years older than herself, smiled.

A huge bonfire filled the glade, its heat hitting her immediately. Garlands of holly, ivy and laurels draped snowy branches, each one linked by lanterns below which an abundance of gifts sat heaped. Laden tables sagged under the weight of the treats that they held, treats that Anna had never seen before. Each was set at different heights for the many different creatures gathered around.

Foxes celebrated with rabbits, wild cats with mice, wolves with deer.

The child had never seen such a sight.

The eyes grew even wider at the sight of a teenage boy jumping joyfully from tree to tree, hitting snow off branches as he did – much to the annoyance of the animals gathered underneath, who were soon coated in a fresh dusting of white. He looked no more than eighteen in human years and was dressed from head to foot in green, his face covered in leaves; she had never seen the like.

"Greetings Mother Christmas, you are just in time for the burning of the Yule log," a large ox announced as it approached, eyeing the girl with disdain.

Anna's mouth dropped open, not believing her ears. An animal who could talk?!

"I see that you bring a visitor from the land of man."

"Anna is my friend, Aurochs."

"Can humans *ever* be our true friends, Mother Christmas?" He glared at the girl but said no more on the matter.

Anna suddenly felt rather unwelcome. A comforting hand on her shoulder eased her.

"All is well."

Her companion smiled and moved closer to the fire.

Before Anna could say anything, a light appeared catching her attention. It swiftly exploded into a luminous mass, almost too bright to bear. The girl scrunched her eyes up against the glare as the light mass split and each part darted around her in a frantic rush, this way... that way... all over. She could not work out who – or what – they were. The thought was snatched from her as a dull hum filled the night sky.

Animals fell silent in an instant, their chatter and merrymaking cut short.

With a swish of her companion's hand, the bonfire and lanterns extinguished, leaving only thin trails of smoke floating skywards.

"DANGER!"

Anna herself then cried out, startled at a small tree that sprang to life beside her. Shock joined astonishment as the tree stood up on two legs, reminding her of a wizened old witch.

Her companion spoke.

"Madam Spriggan, you are awake!"

The Spriggan shook its head angrily. "Not through choice, Mother Christmas! Once again, humans bring fear, our ancient traditions thwarted by their need to destroy. Heed me, FLEE! *FLEEEE!*"

At these words, the mass of lights extinguished, as if a lightbulb had suddenly been switched off. The woods were now engulfed in complete darkness, so black that it was hard to see your hand in front of you.

The hum grew ever louder overhead, like angry thunder and lighting. The animals fled in different directions. Anna clamped her hands to her ears to block out a deafening roar that screamed above, while the trees jarred below. The Spriggan followed suit, disappearing on the icy wind...

What felt like a never-ending eternity then slowly diminished, the deafening roar returning to its previous hum. The howl of an air raid warning that carried far over the frozen land replaced it. Flak exploded and a cacophony of fireworks followed, the night sky lighting up as bright as the sun as the bombs dropped. Even at this distance, the ground shook.

Her companion grasped her hand.

"We must go!"

In the blink of an eye, they vanished.

Present Day

The ground shuddered violently. Huge trucks rumbled past like carriages on a train, all going in the same noisy direction. An old man, skin ravaged by years in the African sun, gripped onto his walking stick for dear life. He was not the only one.

Unbeknownst to him, a host of animals scurried back to their dens fearful of what was occurring, the peace of the ancient woodland shattered.

"Nothing for you to worry about, Mr Harper-Fox." Steve Wyatt reassured.

Hard eyes glared at the American, in his smart Madison Avenue suit. A taller gentleman wearing a large cowboy hat stood at his side. It was a strange sight to see in the middle of the English countryside.

The lofty companion spoke, a low Texan drawl filling the air.

"Just a minor hiccup with transport, sir!"

A gravelly voice hissed, "It'd better be! If the villagers get wind of this, we've had it."

"Trust me, it will all be done and dusted before anyone can go to war. Everyone will be richer. Everyone will be happier."

Shrewd eyes squinted. Those pale blue orbs had seen many things during their long life, some good, some bad. Now they looked content, knowing soon that all their troubles would be over. "You mean *we'll* be richer and happier?!'"

"Just as it should be!" Steve Wyatt chuckled.

The eyes narrowed to slits. "I don't like you."

Wyatt shifted uncomfortably. "Luckily, sir, we are not here to be friends – just to make one another richer!"

"Idiot!"

Wyatt bit his tongue. It would give him great pleasure tearing a strip off this rude, inbred Limey. But he had such a tough hide that it wouldn't even register. He must think of the money, the fat bonus that awaited him if he could just pull this off. The Bahamas, a new car, maybe an apartment overlooking Central Park...

This 'Limey' was as greedy as he was. On the hook, almost there, one signature and they could leave this godforsaken backwater for good... and never see old misery guts again! A smile cracked his lips at the thought.

More trucks thundered past.

"While these guys ship out," Wyatt shouted over the racket, "we could discuss any worries that you may still have over coffee at Frankly Hall?"

"No!" Harper-Fox snapped. "My housekeeper will see two yanks, one looking as if he's just climbed down from a horse and the other one like he's just stepped off a runway, then the news of your visit will be around the village like wildfire.

Wyatt's eyes filled with hate. The taller Texan shook his head in warning, speaking quickly.

"We can discuss the matter further at our hotel. Hopefully get an agreement in place, and then begin."

"*If* the money is right," Harper-Fox scowled.

"I'd expect no less!" the Texan laughed.

"Let's get this formalized, sir." Steve Wyatt moved quickly towards a black limousine parked at the edge of the woods. "The car is just here."

The glare was back again. "I'm not blind! My body may have diminished, but the brain is still as sharp as a tick."

Wyatt cursed silently. Calling this misery 'Scrooge' would be apt... though redemption would not happen, even should a hundred ghosts visit the bad-tempered grouch.

"Only when you reach old bones will you understand that though we're not as quick as you young whipper-snappers, we're immensely brighter... fool!"

He'd had enough. Wyatt spat his words. "My name is Wyatt, Steve *Wyatt!*"

Harper-Fox clapped. "Bravo, you know your own name!"

If steam could have sprouted from Wyatt's ears, it would have; he could hold it in no longer.

"You pompous, rude, inbred—"

"Gentleman, what does this achieve?" The Texan hastily interrupted. "Let's agree that you both dislike the other, and return to our hotel to discuss what's important."

Wyatt glared at the old curmudgeon, who smirked in response, pleased to have gotten a rise. Both men nodded reluctantly. The chauffeur-driven car pulled quickly away.

The departure was watched closely...

On a distant hill, doe eyes scanned the scene urgently. A magnificent deer, whose antlers stood proud and tall, stamped its hooves and hissed loudly at their parting, sounding like a feral cat. It watched as the car twisted and turned down country lanes until finally out of sight.

Trotting over the brow of the hill, the deer now disappeared.

Six Months Later

A small white car that had seen far better days came to a juddering halt besides tall iron gates. The four people it held stared ahead, wide-eyed.

"This can't be right!"

Simon Harper looked furiously at the map.

The woman sitting next to him pointed to a wooden sign, withered with age and barely visible beneath overgrown ivy. "Frankly Hall."

Simon gulped hard, "So, this *is* it!"

"It seems so," his wife Ella stammered.

A collective gasp filled the car.

"We're going to live here?!" A young boy, no older than ten years, cried.

Both parents nodded as if on autopilot.

An excited, high-pitched shrill erupted beside him. "Can I have a pony?"

Danial glared at his little sister Lily. Fingers were pushed firmly into ears.

The parents nodded again as if struck dumb. The shock of the sight before them hit them like a ton of bricks. Simon stumbled from the car, his wide eyes following a sweeping driveway up towards a large dark house perched on top of a distant hill. A sudden light-headedness made him grip the iron gates as if his life depended on it.

Ella joined him. "Are you OK?"

Simon forced a smile, trying to convince not just his wife, but also himself that everything was going to be fine. He pulled open the gates, which creaked loudly like an old, out-of-tune violin.

"It's just... so... *big!*" It was Ella's turn to wobble. "I never thought..."

Silently, they stared ahead as if locked in some kind of magical trance. The house looked as if it had just stepped out of a gothic fairy tale, its turrets and towers standing proud.

Frankly Hall was tall rather than wide, with small mullioned windows glinting in the low December sun. Even from this distance, it looked huge; a hundred times bigger than the house they'd left that morning.

Lily's excited shouts brought them back to reality with a bump. Simon squeezed his wife's hand. "Shall we?"

Ella raised a brow. "I think so, before Lily implodes!"

Shakily, they walked back to the old white car and drove through the gates. Endless parkland stretched as far as the eye could see, tinged in a fresh coat of frosty white. Higher and higher they trundled, twisting this way and that, their laden car – which contained all their worldly belongings – almost screaming with the strain.

"Come on, Bertie, you can do it!"

"Bertie?" Ella laughed sarcastically.

Simon stroked the dashboard. "Ignore her, my little beauty."

Pedal to the floor, he pushed on.

'Bertie' obeyed, groaning upwards towards the house. With a last concerted effort, clutch burning and bonnet smoking, a loud pop brought the car to a shuddering halt right outside the hall.

Bertie had now well and truly given up.

Ella looked gravely at the smouldering wreck.

"Out, kids... now!"

Simon followed suit, pleased to have reached their destination.

"He'll be fine. I'll fix the old boy tomorrow."

Ella eyed him doubtfully.

Simon took in the house's towering facade and gulped. Up close it looked even grander than it had when down in the valley.

Ella followed his gaze and felt faint. Was this really theirs?

Nervously, she walked behind Simon, Danial and Lily, who climbed up steep steps towards a beautiful stone archway that graced a large front door beyond.

"Key?" Ella spoke impatiently, eager to see what lay behind it.

Simon took a deep breath as he inserted the key. An ominous whine followed as the dark oak slowly creaked open.

Four pairs of eyes took in the large, imposing hallway.

Ella gasped, "Our old house could fit into this one room alone!"

Simon squeezed her hand. His stomach flipped between terror and excitement. If the grandness of the entrance hall was an indicator, this house must have been truly magnificent in its heyday. Now though, the years having passed by, it had clearly seen better times.

Once-fine wallpaper now looked worn and tattered against yellowing paintwork; frayed carpets were tired and old; countless spider webs covered numerous old portraits that hung above a large wooden staircase that wound up into creepy darkness.

The house had not been properly looked after for years, and it showed.

In Simon's stomach, terror won out.

"Why did he leave it to get in such a state?" Ella asked. "He had the money!"

Simon shook his head, not knowing the answer.

"I don't remember seeing him as a child. There was the odd mention of a Great Uncle Tom, the grumpy loner who lived in a big house... but that was all. I never paid much attention, to be honest with you. Maybe he liked things... untouched?"

"The understatement of the year, I'd say." Ella took in the tired surroundings.

"A Christmas Tree!" Lily cried, joyfully running to a fine spruce nestled beneath the staircase.

"It's too early for a Christmas tree." Ella frowned.

"But it has tinsel on it, Mummy."

"One garland does not a Christmas tree make, young lady!"

Ella looked at Simon. "Maybe it's left over from last year?"

"It would be a brown twig by now." Simon touched its leaves. "No, it's fresh." He sniffed the air. "Hmm, Piney!"

Danial looked around them, disgust on his face. "We left our house for *this* dump?" All he could smell was damp and mould. "It's like an old haunted house. Any minute a headless ghost will float down those stairs."

He wanted to go home – *now.*

"*Are* there ghosts here, Mummy?" Lily clung to her mother, who glared at the boy.

"Danial, you're scaring your sister!"

The young boy looked disappointed. He didn't just want to scare Lily but his parents too. Maybe then, they could leave this rubbish tip and return home.

Ella shook her head. "No, baby, it's just an old house, that's all."

"Such a big house..." Simon gulped hard. It was Ella's turn to squeeze *his* hand.

"Your uncle left you a wonderful building. A new home in which our family can grow. We'll make it work."

Danial sneered sarcastically, much to his mum's annoyance.

What had happened to her once-lovely boy? Since he'd found out that they were moving, he had become sullen, moody, angry. He missed his friends, and the place he'd grown up in – she understood that. But this was an opportunity of a lifetime.

Hopefully, the kind boy she knew and loved would come back to them... and the sooner the better.

"You're too young to understand," Ella scolded, "one day you'll appreciate the gift we've been left. This is all *ours,* Danial, not some faceless council's."

"It wasn't *specifically* left to me," Simon continued. "I'm his only living relative."

"Then how lucky are *we!*" Ella beamed.

"*Are* we?" Simon sighed wearily. "The house needs money – which we don't have to spare. We have only just enough to scrape by, after paying off the debts, inheritance tax, solicitor costs..."

"You sound like your son," Ella groaned. "It's *yours,* Simon! Bricks, mortar... and all that comes with it; we'll find a way to make it work."

"*Ours!*" Simon hugged his wife. "Let's explore the place before I change my mind and sprint for the car."

"The car is broken, remember?"

"Ah, so you have arrived?" A soft voice floated down from the darkness, making all four jump, startled. Before they could think, before they could even breathe, an elderly woman descended from the shadows.

Lily clung to her mother. "Are you *sure* there are no ghosts, Mummy?"

For the briefest moment, Ella couldn't speak. The lone figure was as white as a sheet and her dress didn't ease concerns. Old-fashioned clothes made her look like she was from another century.

She stopped before them. "Mr Harper-Fox? I am Mrs Briggs, the housekeeper. Welcome to Frankly Hall."

"Oh... yes, the solicitor *did* say that you would be here," Simon said, moving forward and shaking her hand vigorously. "This is my wife, Ella, and our two children, Danial and Lily."

The three nodded a silent hello. In Danial's world, she looked like a floating phantom beneath her long skirt. He smirked; he must tell Lily that later.

"I have prepared rooms for all of you. Please let me know if you wish to change them though, and I will carry out your wish on the 'morrow".

"'*Morrow?*'" Danial mouthed silently at his father.

A stern look made it snap shut.

"Thank you." Ella nodded.

"They are just at the top of the stairs. You'll forgive me if I don't take you up. Once a day up those steep steps makes my old bones fit to creak."

Danial burst out a laugh. It was Ella's turn to glare; he fell instantly silent.

"I'm sure we'll find them."

"I had started the Christmas tree, but knowing that you have children I've left it for you all to finish. There are some pretty baubles and garlands under the stairs."

"We leave ours until just before Christmas," Simon smiled.

A withering look silenced him.

"The Frankly Hall Christmas tree goes up every first of December and remains standing until the twelfth night. The ritual has survived centuries – surely you respect tradition?"

"Of course!" Simon spluttered, "I meant no offence."

"If you are unhappy with the tree, Joe – the gardener – can fell another one from Frankly Woods, but I'll guarantee you will not find a better specimen."

"We have a *gardener?*" Ella asked.

Mrs Briggs nodded. "Old Joe has been working here nigh on forty years. I have left all the information about the running of the house – and its staff – in your office, sir. Not a lot to read as there's only three of us: Joe, Verity and myself. There *is* a huge stack of post for you to deal with though, sir. Also, countless messages on the answerphone from a Mr Steve Wyatt. He wants to speak to you urgently about some deal or agreement; he's left his number."

"You listened?" Ella asked.

A death-like stare hit her. Mrs Briggs spoke affronted, "I'm not in the *habit* of listening in at private conversations, Madam. I was simply in the office cleaning when the American called."

"American?" Simon exclaimed.

"Yes."

"I'm sorry, I didn't mean..." Ella said, trailing off apologetically.

The stare softened slightly.

"I would leave the post until the morn, sir; get a good night's sleep first."

"We'll deal with it together tomorrow." Ella smiled.

Old eyes grew stern. "Surely, Madam, you will be too busy looking after the children?!"

Ella smarted, indignant. Before she could say something unpleasant, Simon stepped in.

"We *both* take care of our children, Mrs Briggs."

She raised a brow but said no more on the matter.

"For when you have settled in, I have prepared a cold supper for you in the kitchen. The fire is lit as the wind likes to howl through these old passages at night."

"You're leaving?" Ella asked.

"I do not stay past dusk; the house does not like it. Good evening, Mr and Mrs Harper-Fox," the old woman nodded, "children."

Without another word, she walked away, disappearing through a small doorway under the stairs.

"'The house does not like it!'" Ella shook her head bemused, "And those comments... the days when women were chained to the stove have long passed."

Simon smirked, "Mercifully..."

Ella punched him hard on the arm. She was far from the best cook and could even burn water. The smirk quickly disappeared.

"She 'does not stay past dusk!'" Danial threw up his arms and pretended to be a spook. "That's when those ghosts do roam... whoooooo!"

Lily's shrill cry drowned out her brother's laughter.

"Keep this up, young man and you'll be spending the night down here to find out if they really *do* exist!"

The laughter stopped abruptly.

Ella raised a brow. "'Harper-Fox'? What is *that* all about?!"

"The old family name," Simon said sheepishly.

"And you didn't think to mention it at the altar?"

"I've always been a plain old Harper," Simon declared. "I'm *still* just a Harper!"

"So my married name is Ella *Harper-Fox?*"

Simon shook his head, exasperated. "No!"

"Harper-Fox sounds posh!" Danial added, rather unhelpfully.

"And this isn't the council house we left behind this morning, Tonto!" Ella exclaimed.

Danial looked blankly, not a clue what his mother was talking about.

"This is better," Simon smiled.

"As long as there are no ghosts," Lily huffed.

Ella hugged her daughter closer. "Don't fear, there's nothing strange or mysterious about this place."

Chapter One

The morning dawned snowily.

Outside, a crisp winter wonderland sparkled for as far as the eye could see. Everything looked so clean and fresh, the three distant hills on the horizon a dazzling mass of white. They were certainly not in the city anymore.

Danial hated the house. He was tired and yawned loudly. They had moved into this new dump only yesterday, and it had been a long, miserable day. He'd left his home, his friends – everything that he'd ever known – to live in the back of beyond.

His parents, Simon and Ella, had inherited a stupid hall, and now he was stuck here with them and his brat of a younger sister, Lily. They'd also inherited its staff: a housekeeper called Mrs Briggs – a strange woman who talked as if the hall were a living thing ('The house does not like me staying past dusk'), Joe – the old gardener (who he was yet to meet) and a girl called Verity who 'cleaned' occasionally. Judging by the state of the house, 'Verity' had not been there for some time.

Danial's parents were *not* his favourite people.

Frustrated, after breakfast, the boy decided to

explore his new surroundings, starting his quest with gusto. The house – though large – was quicker to inspect than he'd first thought it would. One dark, musty room looked very similar to the last, and soon he was bored. He tried and failed to drown out the shouts from his mum to help Lily with the Christmas tree. Not in any mood to be civil, he slammed shut what turned out to be the library door.

Danial looked around. Leather-clad books stretched from floor to ceiling. Soon however, one book looked very similar to the last...

Gloom grew.

There was nothing to do here.

No one to play with.

But then something caught his eye. A large, smoke-tinged map hung above the fireplace.

Danial read the date: 1752. this map was *old!* Studying it, two points of interest seemed to stand out. The *Illusion Hills* to the north; a trio of peaks, with the largest – *Black Tor Hill* – at its centre. Below this Black Tor Hill, a small river ran, twisting this way and that like a slithering snake. For a moment, Danial pondered the odd name. His musings came to an abrupt halt as his eyes rested on the second feature, 'King Arthur's Burg' to the West.

The boy did not recognize the word, but images of knights and swordfights flooded his young mind. Excitement grew; maybe it was not so bad here after all? He followed its route with his finger. If he could just reach there...

Taking the plunge, Danial hurried outside, ignoring the cries from his mum. He glared up at the house, now considering it his nemesis. The hall looked grand sitting there, with its towers and turrets worthy of a fairy-tale castle. Yet looks were deceiving; inside was a shell. Tittering to himself, he'd make sure he told Lily all about the spooks later.

Still looking up at the Hall, Danial gulped hard. Intricate stone carvings peered down at him as if judging his every move. A day with his sister would make them see things from his point of view. Two huge ravens on top of the roof, wings outstretched, seemed about to swoop down at any moment to chase him away. The boy did not need to be told twice. He hurried quickly down the stone steps, freeing himself from the birds' glare.

Three tall hills stood proud ahead, the narrow river below glistening in the autumn sunshine. Today, with its surface covered in white, Black Tor Hill's appearance did not match its name. The endless parkland that surrounded the house looked no different; Old Father Frost held the land firmly in its grip.

Raising his right arm towards the rising sun – as the Boy Scouts had taught him, Danial knew that he was facing north. He figured out which way was west but could not see anything remotely interesting in the snowy landscape. Initial excitement began to fade rapidly.

Before he could decide whether to head towards the trio of hills ahead or the swathes of seemingly unremarkable ground to the west, Danial's mum came out with a scarf, gloves and a warm coat.

"If you won't help with the tree..."

"I'm not a baby!"

Ella looked stern. "No, but I still think of you as one of my babies!"

Her worried eyes scanned the fresh snowfall. December had never had more appropriate weather. The *Beast from the East* they'd called it on the news; an icy-cold blast that had blown in from Russia with a ferocious bite.

The coat was slipped over Danial's arms and the scarf wrapped snugly around his neck. All attempts to back away failed miserably.

"I want you to stay close to the village today," The gloves were placed firmly on his hands, "just until we get our bearings."

Danial raised his eyes.

"You wouldn't be allowed out today if I didn't have so much to do."

Danial huffed frustratedly and moved down the icy steps.

"Home by one o'clock for lunch, OK? No dawdling or mischief-making!" His mum shouted after him.

The boy sighed deeply. The choice had been made for him.

King Arthur's Burg would have to wait...

Chapter Two

The walk to Frankly Village took longer than Danial had thought it would. Slipping and sliding underfoot, misjudging puddles frozen solid on the ground did not help. Danial would never admit it to his mum, but he was grateful for the coat, gloves and scarf which kept the bitter wind at bay.

The village was smaller than he'd imagined. It had only one main street – Ley Lane – and one shop, whose window twinkled brightly with fairy lights. On either side of the shop were small cottages, each built of the same pale stone. Ahead, he could see an old pub which sat at the far end of the icy thoroughfare.

"The Green Man," read Danial, puzzled as like everything else it was completely covered in white.

Shrugging his shoulders, he moved on. Walking haphazardly, he spotted a village hall and local school – Frankly Primary. Soon, he and Lily would start there, but not until January. Danial smiled at the thought of a whole month off, thoughts of exploration and adventures taking away any sensible ones that tried to force their way in.

Aimlessly, he wandered back the way he came.

His attention was soon brought back to the shop, the *Frankly Post Office and Store*. The twinkling lights in its window illuminated a huge selection of Christmas goodies. Outside, he read a notice on the wall—

Frankly Christmas Fair
Saturday 12th December
Frankly Village Hall
Doors open at 11 am

—but was soon bored again.

Danial's greedy eyes wandered back to the rich display. Though still full from breakfast, he could always squeeze in a chocolate bar. As he entered the shop, a small bell rang out and the heat hit him immediately. For a few moments, he savoured the warm glow that began to thaw out his now-frozen bones.

"May I help you?"

A woman, aged around forty, came in to view. Danial pointed to the largest chocolate bar in the window.

"That please?"

Sneering laughter followed his words and for the first time, he saw them – two young boys were sniggering at the end of one of the aisles.

"One pound, please." The shopkeeper held out her hand, the other holding firmly onto the chocolate bar as if at any moment he might snatch it and flee from the shop.

Danial rummaged in his coat for his money.

"I've not seen you around here before. Are you on holiday?"

He shook his head. "We moved in yesterday. I live at Frankly Hall."

"Ah," the shopkeeper smiled knowingly, "my sister Verity works there in the holidays... and Mrs Briggs did confirm your arrival yesterday."

"She's the housekeeper and Verity cleans," Danial replied, to the amusement of the two boys.

"Yes. You know, gossip spreads like wildfire when a new owner takes over the hall. What's your name?"

"Danial... Danial Harper."

The boys fell into hysterics.

"Well, my name is Veronica Michaels; I own the shop." She pointed to the laughing duo. "The two giggling fools over there are Nathan and Freddy Davies, Flynn's boys. Flynn owns Butler's Farm, just beyond the woods. I'm sure that you will meet some *sensible* children when you start at school, rather than ones silly enough to laugh at a strange accent."

Both scowled at him.

Danial looked quickly away.

The shopkeeper continued, oblivious. "They've never been the same since their mother passed, God bless her. Flynn's too busy with his farm to watch them properly, so they run wild; as feral as they come."

Danial could well believe it. He would stay well away from these two boys.

Veronica handed him the chocolate bar but refused his money.

"Call it a welcome gift."

"Thank you," Danial nodded. He waved the chocolate bar in farewell and left the shop.

Heavy snowflakes had begun to fall again, making the icy landscape even whiter, if such a thing were possible.

But the loud sniggering was back, this time behind him – Nathan and Freddy Davies had followed him outside. The chocolate bar was wrenched violently from his hand.

"Give it back!" Danial cried.

Freddy mimicked his accent, roaring with laughter. Nathan sneered menacingly. "Take it!"

He did not move.

"Thought not, *chicken!*" Nathan laughed and began to imitate a clucking hen. He tore open the chocolate bar and bit a huge chunk out of it.

Anger welled up inside Danial like a volcano ready to erupt. Without thought of the consequences, he shoved Nathan hard. The bully hit the pavement, sliding on ice. The chocolate flew skywards; Danial caught it and ran.

An angry roar filled the air behind him. *"GET HIM!"*

Danial didn't stop to look back, running as fast as his legs would carry him. Ahead was a mass of trees. If he could *just* reach them...

Bellowing shouts and chasing footsteps followed; it felt as if spiteful hands would pull him back to his doom at any moment now. Danial fled deep into the woods, ducking this way and that, large branches and twigs scratching at his clothes and he feared each one might be the grip that held him firm... until, at last, he finally lost his pursuers.

Stooping down low in the undergrowth, he tried to catch his breath, icily visible before him like a willow-the-wisp in the gloom.

"You think you got away?" Nathan's mocking sneer accompanied a howl of chill wind that gusted through the trees like the cry of a banshee. "We'll find you!"

Danial shivered not just with cold but also fear. He couldn't see where the threat came from, but it felt like it filled every nook and cranny. His heart pounded hard in his chest. Despite the bitter chill, his insides burned like fire. Hot tears stung his cheeks, and anger towards his parents rather than his bullies now raged unabated. *They* wanted their new life and *he* was stuck here, paying the consequences in an awful dump of a house. Worse still... he was now stuck with Nathan and Freddy Davies!

For what felt like an age, he did not move, did not dare to breathe. The only noise came from the odd wild animal scurrying back to its den. Finally, his frozen limbs protesting angrily, Danial fled deeper into the wildwood, taking his chances.

Numerous pathways and trails shot off around him and soon he was completely lost. The boy did not care though, as long as it was as far away as possible from his pursuers. The shopkeeper had called them 'wild', and he knew these kind of bullies when he saw them; he was not going to be their next victim.

The ground suddenly fell away sharply. In slow motion, Danial flipped mid-air, the chocolate bar flying skywards; a sickening thud followed. For a moment he lay there, trying to catch his breath. Then the pain hit, snatching away what little remained. He could see that his ankle was resting at a strange angle. A foggy haze replaced the painful throbbing and slowly his eyes began to close.

A face suddenly came into view above... and then was gone.

Chapter Three

The boy stirred.

Warmth at his side crackled and spat, a fire lighting up the shadows. Its comforting heat tried to lull him back to peaceful slumber, a calm engulfing him. He may hate his new house, but at least his bed was comfort—

Then he remembered.

Danial's eyes shot open and he sat bolt upright. Taking in a stone roof, he realised he was in some sort of cave. Large icicles hung from the ceiling, others shot up haphazardly from the ground. This was *not* his bedroom.

A distant glow like the light at the end of a tunnel sparkled in the dull gloom. Beyond was a small opening, the snow still falling heavily outside. The boy became puzzled as he looked down; a fur blanket covered him from chest to toe. Then he remembered the pain...

For a moment Danial sat still, hardly daring to breathe. His earlier agony was still fresh in his mind and he did not want a repeat performance. Strangely though, he felt nothing.

No painful throbbing.

No discomfort.

Gingerly he moved his foot.

Nothing.

Danial pulled the fur from his foot; his eyes growing ever wider. His ankle looked perfectly normal, not strange at all. He echoed his actions with the right one, just in case.

Both looked the same.

"You are awake?"

Startled, he jolted backwards.

A young girl came in to view; just a little taller than he was and dressed from head to foot in fur except for a bright white cape which cascaded from her shoulders down to the ground. Danial guessed that she was no older than eighteen years.

"Who are you?" He gulped hard, stammering warily.

Doe eyes blinked at him. "I'm Cervanae. You fell in the woods... I helped you."

Suspicious eyes locked with hers. He'd been warned countless times about 'stranger danger'.

"Do not fear, all is well." The girl spoke as if reading his mind.

"Where is this place?"

"The old hollow."

Her answer did nothing to ease his concerns. Danial made to get up, but fell back onto a fur pillow. A wave of fatigue swept over him like a thick fog creeping over the land. Cervanae spoke gently.

"You still heal and must rest a while longer."

"I hurt my ankle," yet he moved it back and forth easily. "What happened?"

"Nature, Danial, son of Simon."

He blinked, shocked.

"You know my name *and* my father's?"

"Word spreads fast when a new owner takes over the land."

A strange, drowsy thought came to him. This girl was only slim and slight. How did he get into this cave?

"My friends helped."

Again he blinked, shocked. She'd answered his question before he'd even asked it!

He stared around doubtfully.

"Where are they?"

"They have returned to their homes in the wildwood."

"I don't remember seeing—"

"They do not live in a dwelling with which you would be familiar." The girl tutted, exasperated. "You ask far too many questions and must sleep to recover your strength."

Danial shook his head, yawning loudly. "No. Mum and Dad will be worried, I have to go!"

Cervanae rummaged through her cape, which sparkled and glowed in the firelight. She brought out a small, shining goblet from her pocket.

"Then drink this. When you awake, you will be fully recovered and ready to return to your parents at Frankly Hall."

"I'm fine." Danial fought to keep his eyes open, his suspicions aroused once again.

"Your body is weak."

Danial mulled over her words. He felt as if he'd just run a marathon, though aged only ten years and never having run a marathon, he was only guessing as to what it must be like to run twenty-six miles. He was completely and utterly drained.

Cervanae handed him the goblet. "The potion is powerful and takes time to work."

Though still a stranger, she *had* helped him...

Gingerly, he took a sip.

A huge smile spread across his face. It tasted of strawberries, bubble gum and candyfloss... all the good things mixed together.

"You must drink it down in one for the magic to do its job."

"Magic?"

"Nature's magic."

Still none the wiser, Danial obeyed. A comforting warmth filled him, moving gradually from the top of his head to the tip of his toes.

His weary eyes closed once more.

Chapter Four

The large grandfather clock that stood proud in Frankly Hall struck half-past-one.

Ella's eyes grew narrow. That old clock must be at least a hundred years old and was sure to be wrong. She checked her watch carefully, puffing out her disappointment – within a minute or so, it was correct.

Ella stepped outside, her eyes scanning the horizon which gleamed pure white under the fresh falling of snow. She cursed herself for letting Danial go out exploring. Again, she checked her watch, hoping that she had made some kind of mistake.

Turning back towards the house, her shout, "SIMON!" reverberated through the old hallways,

Within a few seconds, her husband had joined her on top of the steps, and shivered in the frigid air. "It's coming down heavy now – the kids will be pleased. Proper festive weather for the time of year."

"Danial's late!" Ella spoke as if she had not heard him. She looked at Simon, concern growing in her eyes. "I told him to be back home for lunch at one o'clock."

Simon hugged his wife to him, not just for reassurance, but also to warm his chill body.

"Children and snow... you'll be lucky to see him before Christmas Day!"

"Danial could eat one more potato than a pig. He wouldn't miss lunch for all the snow in the world!"

Simon grew a little worried; Ella was correct. Though there was hardly a pick on him, Danial could wolf down his share and then some.

"Let's go find him."

Disappearing back inside, he reappeared a few moments later with a bundle of coats and scarves. "Mrs Briggs will watch Lily, so... where to?"

"The village." Ella eyed the pristine wonderland, trying to convince herself that everything would be ok. "I told him not to wander far and to stay close to it.'

"Then he's probably met some local village kids and lost track of time," Simon puffed knowingly. "He'll be playing snowballs as we speak."

Ella nodded, trying to stem a rising panic that gripped her insides like a vice. She hoped that Simon was right.

Pushing any negative thoughts away, the couple moved swiftly down the snowy steps and into the icy landscape beyond.

***

"Danial, you must wake."

A soft voice floated gently through the drowsy haze.

The boy snuggled deeper under the warm covers, trying to remember the wonderful dream from which he'd just stirred.

The voice grew more insistent.

"It is Cervanae, you must wake up."

The penny dropped.

Danial's eyes shot open in an instant, taking in the rocky ceiling above. *Still in the cave...*

"We must be swift; your family searches for you as we speak."

Beyond the cave, he could hear his name being called. Each shout grew more urgent than the last.

Cervanae helped him to his feet. Danial stood astounded; the tiredness that engulfed him just moments ago had disappeared completely. He felt as light as a feather, like he could run a marathon for real.

He then remembered his mother's words...

"What time is it?"

"It has just past two o'clock, human time."

He was late! A telling-off was coming. A strange thought took away his worry. *'Human time'* – whatever did she mean? He began to ask, but words caught in his throat.

With a swish of Cervanae's hand, the fire was extinguished.

Danial stumbled over his words, not believing what he was seeing. His previous question was gone in an instant, replaced by a new one. "How did you—"

"Magic."

The boy laughed nervously but grew silent as Cervanae did not seem to get the joke. He followed her to the edge of the cave.

Outside, the snow still fell heavily, the trees swathed in pure white sleeves at least three inches deep. The girl took his hand and moved swiftly beyond the entrance.

The wind blew bitterly, but strangely, he felt an odd warmth course through his body.

An urgent call filled the air once more; even closer this time.

Excitement grew.

"Mum!"

Cervanae led them one way then another, zigzagging quickly through the frozen landscape – so much so that soon the boy was completely lost again. One final dart to the left brought them out at the edge of the wildwood.

Cervanae pointed ahead. "Your parents are yonder."

Two lone figures stood out against the stark white. Danial's earlier anger towards them disappeared in an instant. He made to move.

The girl did not follow. "I need no thanks from your parents, Danial, son of Simon."

Again, Cervanae had answered his question before he'd even asked it.

An urgent shout filled the air once more, this time his father.

"Your parents grow frantic; you must go... *now!*"

"May I visit you again?"

"You are always welcome here."

Danial beamed, walking quickly away. He stopped dead; how would he ever find her again? Turning back, his eyes grew wide at the sight of the stub tail of a deer that quickly disappeared back into the wildwood.

Puzzled, he hurried to where his parents were standing.

Chapter Five

The next day dawned as snowy as the last. The Beast from the East was showing no signs of abating any time soon.

The front doorbell rang during breakfast.

Each looked at another... but everyone was there, all accounted for. Who could it be knocking at such an early hour?

Mrs Briggs's entrance soon answered their question. "A delegation from the village has arrived, sir. I've put them in your office while you finish your breakfast."

"A *delegation?*" Simon replied, mystified.

The old woman nodded.

Curiosity could not wait until Simon had finished his bacon butty; he stood, sandwich in hand, and left the room. Ella followed closely, never having had a 'delegation' in her house before. They entered the office.

A smartly dressed man greeted them enthusiastically, "Good morning, I am Doctor White."

Behind him stood a mishmash of smiling people.

"Good morning to you." Ella nodded, not sure who exactly Doctor White or any of these people were. Her confusion was somewhat cleared up by his next words.

"We would all like to welcome you and your family to Frankly," the doctor continued. "We hope that you're happy here and will become involved in village life."

"You'll be more than welcome!" Veronica Michaels, the lady from the post office added.

Simon nodded, swallowing the last of his sandwich. "Thank you."

"Still as grand," an older gentleman could be heard to say, "just a little rough around the edges." He then winced at a swift elbow to his side.

"Apologies, my husband has no tact," the woman who stood beside him proffered. She stepped forward, shaking both of their hands.

"I'm Shirley Abbott, landlady of the Green Man. My husband, Stanley – otherwise known as 'the man with no filter' – is just there," she added, rolling her eyes.

Ella laughed, "He speaks the truth. The hall *is* a little rough around the edges."

"It never used to be!" a brusque voice interrupted. "My grandfather attended many tenant balls with the local milord. The house was beautiful then, not at all like it is today."

"That was a *long* time ago, Flynn," said Doctor White.

"It was before his uncle took over, when times were good."

"This is no time for recriminations, Flynn," Veronica added. "You should not speak ill of the dead."

"I told him often enough when he was alive!" Flynn scoffed. "The nasty, old misery guts—"

Veronica nervously intervened, "As you may gather, your uncle was not... particularly well-liked."

"There was nothing *likeable* about him!" Flynn spat.

"I'd have to agree," Stanley Abbott nodded. "Not a greedier nor more spiteful man would you ever meet."

"*As* Veronica said," Doctor White interrupted, "we're not here to crucify the late Mr Harper-Fox, but to welcome the *new* residents to Frankly Hall." He smiled at Simon and Ella, "I do apologise."

This 'welcome meeting' was far from what the two had expected.

"I never knew my uncle," Simon said, breaking the uneasy silence that had descended like a cloud of thick smog.

"And you can't help to whom you are related," added Ella, before swiftly changing the subject. "Tea, anyone?"

Her offer went down a treat, the strategy working perfectly. She began to count heads: Doctor White, Flynn, Shirley and Stanley Abbott, Veronica, and two others who had yet to open their mouths. She moved towards the door, stating "I'll go help Mrs Briggs."

Simon glared at her. He did not want to be left alone with these complete strangers!

"We won't be long," Ella glared back. "Tea for nine."

"What about me?" Mrs Briggs cried. "I *am* a villager as well."

Ella inwardly sighed. "Tea for ten it is then!"

Now happy, Mrs Briggs followed her from the room.

***

Simon huffed his uneasiness. He was finding it hard to think of something else to say, so instead just listened. Fifteen minutes had been and gone and Ella was *still* not back with the tea. Any moment now, he decided, he would make his excuses, run from the room and go find her. 'Won't be long'... codswallop!

Just then, the office door opened.

Never in Simon's life was he so happy to see his wife.

"We thought you'd left us!" Simon took the heavy tray, sighing with both frustration and relief.

"We couldn't find any biscuits!"

"If you ever leave me alone with strangers again, I'll... I'll... divorce you!" Simon whispered under his breath.

Ella gave him a look that said she *hoped* he was joking, then smiled and poured each person a cup of tea; soon all had been served.

Conversation then thankfully flowed; Ella was much better with strangers than Simon ever could be. She talked about the village, the school, and their own plans for the hall. She listened intently and gave helpful suggestions and solutions as each person spoke of the different problems that they themselves faced. She was a true diplomat in the making!

As talk naturally came to a break, Veronica announced, "We have brought you a welcome gift for your front door," as she unwrapped the most beautiful holly wreath, decorated in a mass of festive colours. "I make them from what I can forage in Frankly Woods. As it's Christmas time, we thought that it would be an apt gift for the old hall."

Ella looked amazed. "It's truly beautiful; thank you."

Veronica blushed.

"Veronica has hidden talents," Doctor White agreed, "a true artist."

She blushed more.

"You've all been so kind," Ella said as she smiled at the villagers.

"You're one of us now." Shirley beamed.

Chapter Six

"And where do *you* think you're going?"

Danial came out of his bedroom, quickly buttoning his coat. "Just... out, Mum."

His parents did not believe his tale of broken bones, his rescue by a girl named Cervanae, and all else that had transpired the previous day. He now had to prove to himself that he'd not imagined it all.

"*Out* like last time, when you went missing?"

"I did not go *missing!*" Danial puffed, frustrated. "I fell and hurt myself and was helped by—"

"You *say* you hurt yourself," Ella chided, "yet I can't see a single bruise or scratch on you!"

"Cervanae helped me!"

"Oh, the mysterious girl you spoke of yesterday," Ella said, then after pondering for a moment, "yet no one else here has even mentioned her existence!"

"I broke my ankle; she healed me."

"Danial, that's impossible. You were only gone for three hours."

Danial was growing more and more exasperated with his mother's tone. He didn't know why, but he was desperate for her to believe him.

If only he would be honest about simply staying out too long, Ella wished. But instead he had come up with this clearly ridiculous story and now she'd had enough of his lies. "Come on, coat off young man!" Ella demanded, in a manner that the young boy did not hear often.

"But Mum, she healed me, using... magic!" He spoke carefully, trying to get his words right. "Not like a magician, but... sort of... nature's magic!"

Ella stood unmoved.

"Mum, I just want to *thank* her!"

"Coat. *Now!*"

The fierce look in her eyes told Danial that she would not budge. His coat now came off in a temper and he hurled it straight at his mother.

"We'll have no more of *that* behaviour either," she scolded.

"She *helped* me," the young boy cried. "Is it so wrong to say thank you?!"

"Of course not," Ella said as she folded the coat neatly, "but you don't get rewarded for lies."

"Lies?"

"You disappeared yesterday without so much as a 'goodbye', you were so late for lunch you made both me and your father worry, and instead of admitting you lost track of the time, you come back with this... *fantastical* excuse." Ella shook her head in disbelief. "A girl living in a cave in the woods who heals broken bones with magic?"

"But that's what happened!" Danial protested.

"You will stay in this house until you tell me the truth and admit what you *really* got up to yesterday."

"I *am* telling the truth!"

"No. No more nonsense!" his mother cried exasperatedly. "Since the moment we told you about moving here, you've become a little monster. I won't have it!"

"But I told you! Two boys chased me into the woods. I fell and hurt—"

"Enough!" Ella Cried. "As I have said; lie and you stay inside, the truth and *then* you can go out."

Danial stomped back into his room, slamming the door hard.

Chapter Seven

An insistent knock brought a scowl to Mrs Briggs's face. She shook her head; people had no patience anymore.

Having made it to the front door, she opened it and eyed the two gentlemen standing outside with some suspicion. Behind them, a long black car seemed to take up the whole of the drive. A chauffeur sat still and upright as an inactive robot in the front seat.

The taller of the two men was wearing some type of large cowboy hat. This might be normal in certain American states, but certainly not in rural England. He removed it, nodded his head, and spoke in a long drawl, "Good morning, ma'am."

"Americans?" Mrs Briggs stated sharply.

The Texan chuckled, "That indeed we are." He held out his hand. "Please let me introduce myself; my name is—"

"We don't want any of that *'save your soul'* rubbish here! Try at the church in Frankly Village." She slammed the door shut.

Both men looked at one another.

The shorter one, dressed in a smart Madison Avenue suit, sighed exasperatedly.

"Don't you just *love* these country yokels?"

"*I'm* a country yokel," replied his taller companion.

The younger man stiffened. "Of course sir, I meant no offence."

"None was taken."

Wyatt sighed, relieved. He must *never* upset the boss. Now it was his turn to knock.

The door flew open.

"I *cannot* spend my day opening doors! It's like being back in the war... you were all a nuisance then, too!"

"Please forgive us, ma'am," the Texan begged, "we apologise for interrupting your day, but we have an appointment with your husband, *Mr* Harper-Fox. My name is Henry Carney; I own Shale Oil." He held out his hand.

Mrs Briggs did not take it. "He is *not* my husband!"

"Son?"

"Not that, neither!"

For a moment there was complete silence, the old woman forthcoming with no more information for the two men. To her, one looked as if he's just climbed down from his horse and the other having come from the catwalk of a fashion show.

It was Henry Carney who broke the awkward stand-off. "Is Mr Harper-Fox at home?"

The door slammed shut again, much to his companion's frustration.

"This is just ridiculous!" He knocked again, harder.

"Calm down, Stevie boy!" Carney replaced the cowboy hat on top of his head. "I kinda like their weird ways. It's quaint!"

"Backwoods, more like!" Steve Wyatt sighed deeply, trying to control his growing anger. He had to think of the money, the fat bonus that awaited if he could just pull this off. He allowed his mind to wander in order to overcome the building rage. He had big plans, and no wizened old hag was going to stop them.

Carney chuckled. Before he could say anything further however, the door flew open again.

"Hello! Welcome to England, gentlemen. I am Simon Harper." He shook both of their hands vigorously. "I do hope that your journey was not too tiring?"

"We've flown twelve hours, taken our life in our hands on your freeways and down the winding country lanes, but still found that all easier than trying to see you as scheduled today once we arrived at your home, Mr Harper-Fox."

"I do apologise." Simon sighed. "Our housekeeper is *very* thorough; she's not a great fan of strangers."

Ah, thought the Texan, *now it all makes sense...*

"Is all well, Mr Harper?"

Simon jumped as the old lady re-appeared directly behind him. He nodded, "Yes; these gentlemen are my guests, Mrs Briggs. They have an appointment."

He ushered the two men inside the towering hallway, much to her horror.

"Wow, so grand!" Carney complimented as he looked around the huge entrance room. To him, history seemed to drip from every crack and crevice; it felt like being in Buckingham Palace. "We've never made it to the Hall before, so it's a real treat to be here now."

"Wonderful. Do follow me," Simon replied and led the way to his office. The two men obeyed, closely shadowed by the distrustful housekeeper, who clearly thought that they'd run amok at any moment.

"So dated and worn..." Wyatt muttered.

They reached the small cluttered room and followed Simon inside.

"Would you like some tea, gentlemen?"

"I think that we are all 'tea'd' out," Carney smiled, "though, I wouldn't turn down a glass of whatever is in that decanter."

"A relic from my distant relative; I'm not a big drinker myself."

"Relic or no relic it'll do the job," Henry Carney laughed.

Simon nodded, ushering the old woman from the room. "That will be all for now, Mrs Briggs."

"If you are sure. There *is* strength in numbers, sir!"

"I *am* sure, yes!" He closed the door behind him.

Curiosity got the better of Mrs Briggs.

She pressed her ear firmly against the dark wood.

She did not like what she heard.

Her heart pounding hard in her chest, the full details of the conversation beyond the door began to sink in. *They wouldn't dare, would they?* She straightened up and stepped away from the office door just in time to see Ella appear on the sweeping staircase.

"Mrs Briggs, are you alright? You look as white as a ghost!"

Preoccupied with the mass of thoughts swirling through her brain, the housekeeper did not even hear her name being said. Quickly she scurried away through the servant's door under the stairs.

Ella rolled her eyes at the perceived snub.

"Charming!" She muttered to herself. What was the matter with everyone this merry morn?

She reached the bottom of the stairs and hung up Danial's coat. Guilt now poured over her like a wave... he only wanted to go out and play like any boy his age. But, how could she let him do that with lies still coming from his mouth?

Broken bones healed by magic... *really!*

She had to hold firm until Danial told her the truth about what happened yesterday. And Mrs Briggs's rudeness wouldn't bother her either; Ella would just ignore the batty woman.

Things had admittedly been hectic and somewhat disorganised since they had arrived. But surely there had to be some rules, some boundaries? Mrs Briggs worked for *them,* not the other way around.

In her current state of mind, ignoring the house-keeper was not an option. Determined, Ella headed down the narrow set of steps that led toward the kitchen. Her stomach churned; she was not keen on confrontation.

Mrs Briggs was putting on her coat as Ella reached the bottom step.

"Are you going somewhere?" she asked.

"Yes!" the older woman snapped coldly, the over-heard conversation still raw in her mind.

"Is everything OK?" Ella was building up the courage to challenge her.

"Do you care?" a stony voice snapped back.

Ella tried to hold her temper. "What's wrong?"

"As if you don't know," Mrs Briggs scolded.

Ella stood mouth agape, mystified.

"You think that you can come into our village and change it? Never!"

"I don't under—"

The furious woman stomped out through the backdoor without another word.

Ella stood on its threshold, still none the wiser. "Will you be back today?" She enquired.

No reply was forthcoming.

Enough is enough, she'll have to go, Ella thought.

***

Danial slammed from one side of his room to the other angrily. How could he make his mother believe him?

He *had* been hurt in the forest. Cervanae *had* helped him. It *did* happen…

…didn't it?

He flopped hard onto his bed, frustration getting the better of him. The bed was big and old and reminded him of a sledge… and yet it was nothing compared to his parents'. Their huge four-poster reached from floor to ceiling, at least twelve feet tall. Curtains hung on either side, topped with a canopy above to keep in the warmth. To Danial it was reminiscent of a sailing ship riding mighty waves; a bed fit for a king, even…

He lay there, now really beginning to doubt himself and what really had occurred the previous day.

Perhaps his mother was right. How can a broken ankle be healed in just a few short hours?

He was *sure* he'd seen Cervanae use this 'natures magic', but could he have banged his head and imagined the whole thing?

Danial's head was spinning from truth to lie in equal measure. He lay on his bed pondering, before eventually coming to a conclusion of sorts. Unsure of what had gone on he may be, but he was definitely *not* a liar.

Until his mum accepted this however, he had been told to stay there and not move.

It was going to be a long and boring day.

Chapter Eight

"Exciting news!"

Simon crashed into the large sitting room.

"OK..." Ella looked at him suspiciously.

He paced back and forth, barely able to contain himself. "I didn't want to get anybody's hopes up. Not until I was sure..."

"Tell us, Daddy, tell us!" Lily jumped up excitedly, sharing the sudden joy. "Are we going on holiday?"

Simon walked over and ruffled her hair.

"Yes! And once it's signed, sealed and delivered, *you* can pick the place!"

"Simon, stop filling her head with nonsense," Ella scolded angrily, "we can't afford—"

"Disneyland!" Lily cried.

"Disneyland it is!"

Simon swung Lily around in a merry dance, ignoring his wife's growing scowl. "Where's Danial?"

"In his bedroom, sulking because—"

But Simon was half way up the stairs before Ella could finish her sentence. She huffed in frustration whilst Lily was still dancing around the room. Within a few minutes, he returned with the still-sulking boy.

"I want to go to back my room!" Danial said as he tried to sidestep his father.

He lost the battle.

"We're going to Disneyland!" Lily's cries filled his ears, much to his bemusement.

"Danial, why don't you run down to the cellar and see if you can find the printing press that produces money? Oh, sorry, no, it seems that your father has gone potty!"

Simon skipped over to his wife and planted a kiss on top of her head. "We don't *need* a printing press, not when we have Shale Oil!"

"Who?" The chorus of voices spoke as one.

"My meeting this afternoon, the messages left on the telephone!"

"The *Americans?"* Ella said.

"Not just Americans, *rich* Americans!" He hugged his wife to him. "They've offered us a deal... and I've accepted."

Ella looked aghast. "You've sold the hall?"

Simon shook his head vigorously. "No, *no!"*

Ella sighed deeply, not able to figure out the reason for the strange relief that she felt. This ramshackle place was barely standing. Its musty old rooms, worn furniture, and portraits of complete strangers, all having seen better days. Yet for some unknown reason, she had already grown quite fond of this run-down shack with all its odd nooks and strange crannies.

However rough and ready Frankly Hall might appear, it was *theirs*.

"They want gas. *Shale* gas!"

Relief turned to confusion. "What?"

Simon continued as if he had not heard her. "They're going to pay us a huge amount to let them excavate the surrounding land! We might even get enough to buy our *own* Disneyland!"

Lily shrieked with joy. Danial stuck his fingers into his ears to block the din.

"What do you mean by *'excavate'?*" Ella looked at him quizzically.

"They want to sink a well to search for shale gas"

"Shale Gas?" Ella repeated, still none the wiser.

"It's called fracking," Simon cried excitedly, "and we're going to reap the rewards."

Ella looked concerned. "Isn't fracking supposed to be dangerous?"

"I thought so too initially; I was adamant against it. But the gentlemen explained the process – and believe me, there are minimal risks." Simon looked like he had swallowed a box of fireworks, his radiant excitement abating not one bit. "They'd been dealing with my late uncle regarding the siting of a test well; they were near to completion when he died."

"A *well?*" Ella appeared unconvinced. "What if the children fall down it?!"

"They'll have on-site security, so falling down any well would be impossible. It won't be near the hall anyway; they want to site the well in Frankly Woods."

"No!" Danial exclaimed, horrified.

Simon raised an eyebrow.

"The woods serve no real purpose and they're far enough away from the Hall that we won't be disturbed, not even one bit!"

"People live there, Dad!" Danial cried aghast.

"I don't know where you've got that from Danial; no one lives there," Simon responded unabashedly. "I'm sure that all the rats and mice will happily find another place to live!"

"But Cervanae... and her friends..."

"Oh not *this* again!" Ella said, frustration clear in her voice. "I thought a morning stuck in your room would have knocked some sense into you."

"You *can't* destroy the woods, Dad!" Danial persisted, ignoring his mother. "It's their home."

Simon shook his head. "I've walked the entire estate and didn't see a single person living in the woods." His voice softened just a little. "This is our home Danial, and it would be awful to lose it. When your great, great whatever died, we had to settle his debts, pay inheritance tax... even a 'free' house comes with a whole bucket of financial responsibilities, you know."

"Simon, I don't think the children need to hear about all of that."

"But I think they *do,* Ella." Simon contradicted. "Money doesn't grow on trees, and if sacrificing Frankly Woods is the price we have to pay to stay here, then we don't really have another choice."

"And you are *sure* that there are no risks?" Ella asked, still wary.

"There's *minimal* risk." Simon began to usher Lily and an irate Danial from the room. "Which I shall tell you about when these two leave us in peace. Go play."

"Inside only!" Ella looked sternly at their son.

"But, Dad!" the young boy protested. "You can't—"

"I can and I will!"

A leaflet was placed in Danial's hand.

"Read this."

Before the door closed however, a warning for both children left Simon's lips.

"This is our secret. *No one* must know about it until it's all settled. Do you understand?"

Lily nodded.

Danial looked at the leaflet in his hand – *The Benefits of Fracking: A New Age in Energy*. He stomped up the stairs with it and slammed his bedroom door.

***

"Minimal risk?" Ella asked, concerned.

"It's really nothing for you to worry about."

She raised an eyebrow. "I do worry that all hell tends to break loose whenever fracking is mentioned!"

"Look, the Health and Safety Executive overlooks all aspects of a fracking site. They keep it safe, ensure it's all regulated."

"That doesn't help," Ella replied.

"Anyone wishing to undertake exploration for shale gas must notify them of any well design, including all proposed operational plans before the drilling begins"

"Drilling?"

"There won't be any problems," Simon said softly as he held his wife's hand. "The HSE – as those in the business call it – meet with the operator and inspect their wells to advise them of their legal responsibilities and site safety obligations."

"It all sounds very complicated," Ella sighed.

"It's really not; it'll be perfectly straightforward, I promise."

She still looked doubtful.

Simon puffed out his cheeks in frustration. "Read this!" he said, and handed her the same leaflet that he had given to Danial. "It explains everything."

Ella eyed the pamphlet dubiously. Then, for what seemed like an age to her impatient husband, she read the information contained within from start to finish.

Finally, she looked up at Simon.

"Well?" He was hovering like an eager child waiting for a Christmas present. In the silence his trepidation had grown tenfold.

"I understand about the HSE inspecting any well and a final consent is then given by the Oil and Gas Authority, but I'm still worried. The pamphlet mentions harmful gases, water pollution and earthquakes... they're not '*minimal*' risks!"

"Any company who operates a fracking site must minimize the release of toxic gases as a condition of their license from the Department of Energy and Climate Change. The Environment Agency monitors any ecological concerns regarding shale gas production, and all fracking companies must comply with their laws. The UK government is also currently developing regulations to manage any environmental health risks. So... the real chances of an earthquake actually happening are pretty much the same as you seeing the Loch Ness Monster!"

"But it says they *can* happen?"

"There are strict regulations," Simon hugged Ella towards him. "Risk management is carried out as a norm. I know that you're worried, but you have to trust me, fracking is safe and controlled. It is a cleaner form of energy than fossil fuels like coal, and has potentially huge benefits for the environment. And don't forget the especially good financial benefits for *us!*"

Curiosity got the better of her.

"How *much* financial benefit?"

Simon whispered in her ear.

Her eyes grew wide. *"That much?!"*

"Enough for us to afford to live here for years to come. *And* a secure legacy to leave to the children."

Ella pondered his words, but worry was still winning out.

"It's beyond tempting... but I'm still concerned for the kids. What if they become ill?"

"I'm confident that they *won't*. Please trust me Ella," Simon cried. "If we do this, all our money worries will disappear. So if – or perhaps I should say *when* the roof leaks... well, so what?!"

"I *do* trust you."

"So, it's a green for 'go'?" Simon asked expectantly.

Ella sighed, "I still want to do a lot more research. But from what you have told me, and from reading what the leaflet has to say, it's a *cautious* 'yes'."

Simon swept up Ella in his arms and swung her around. "Our future here is secure!" His sparkling eyes held hers. "I just hope that the villagers can be convinced. The woods skirt the village, so the fracking will be on their doorstep. I don't relish telling them."

"Ah," Ella said, clicking her fingers. "I fear that particular horse may have already bolted."

Simon stared at her blankly.

"Mrs Briggs was standing near the office door when I came downstairs earlier. She was acting very oddly."

Simon groaned. "I'll have a word with her."

"She's already left."

Simon looked confused. "Is she coming back?"

"Your guess is as good as mine. You know, seeing as the subject of Mrs Briggs has now come up, I want to talk to you about her..."

Chapter Nine

A long day was an understatement. Every minute felt like an entire tortuous hour.

Danial had finally made up his mind that he had *not* imagined what had happened to him; the whole thing was real. He now knew that he had to warn Cervanae about the danger to her home, wherever in the forest it may be. But how to find her? The girl lived in Frankly Woods, yes... but *where* exactly he did not know! His anger from earlier had not abated. Most days he did love his parents, but not today. Today, he wished he was an orphan. Their awful 'secret' was going to destroy someone's life!

Hours passed.

No amount of coaxing from his mother or father could shift him from his bed. The wildwoods were going to be destroyed and they did not care one bit.

He felt that it was better to stay in his room, alone.

And he *was* alone.

He was isolated and growing more mad with each passing second. How was he going to warn Cervanae if he was not allowed out?

He must let her know somehow...

Danial wracked his brain and could only think of one solution: he would have to sneak out when everyone else was asleep.

But this plan was easier said than done.

Whilst it was still daytime, he could do nothing but wait. The long, slow seconds turned into even longer minutes, the minutes into never-ending hours.

The boredom of Danial's inaction soon sent him into a deep slumber.

***

What felt like only a few moments later, Danial stirred. Checking his bedside clock he saw that it was only three in the afternoon, but the day appeared as gloomy outside as *he* felt *inside*. The creeping darkness felt like it had even begun to encroach into the room.

What a long, miserable day.

On the mantelpiece above the fireplace in his room sat a small plate of sandwiches and a glass of orange. Lunch left by his parents in their guilt whilst he was asleep, he figured.

Danial's hand rested on top of a book on his bedside table. Frustration with the situation getting the better of him, he picked it up and hurled it across the room.

A loud crash followed. The glass of orange had smashed to the ground, shattering into sharp pieces.

"Oh no," The young boy huffed, despondently climbing from his bed. "More trouble!"

He grabbed a worn t-shirt from the floor, which he used to pick up the broken shards of glass, placing them in a cardboard box which he then dropped in the bin.

As he used some tissues to wipe up the spilt liquid, something wet landed on his neck.

Danial wiped it, wondering how it had gotten there from the floor.

Then a snowflake landed on top of his nose.

He slowly angled his head upwards.

It was *snowing!*

An entire flurry of white powder had now begun to fall. His bedroom ceiling had disappeared, replaced by what appeared to be a dark, leaden sky.

The boy's brain took a few moments to digest and analyse what it was seeing.

How could it be snowing in his bedroom?

Whether his brain could accept the sight or not, it *was* snowing... and snowing heavily at that. His normally dark bedroom furniture was now covered in a fresh dusting of white snow.

Yet for some strange reason, it didn't feel cold. In fact, it was almost as warm as if he was snuggled up in bed. Danial gasped in disbelief as his eyes came to rest on the old sleigh-like bed. A good fifteen centimetres of snow had now settled atop it, the frame's legs barely visible beneath this crisp white blanket. Soon, the wardrobe and a dressing table followed suit, vanishing under the increasingly festive cover.

He *must* be dreaming.

Then a gentle, familiar voice floated in the whiteness.

"Do not fear, Danial, son of Simon; it is I, Cervanae."

Danial blinked snow from his eyes, gasping as she now appeared before him.

Cervanae bobbed her head in greeting.

"You could not leave, so I came to call on you."

Danial was *not* a liar; he had *not* imagined it!

He rubbed his eyes to make sure that she did not disappear; thankfully she did not. A huge smile spread across his face. He stepped forwards and hugged her tightly. Then, for a moment, he stood open-mouthed and silent, unable to find the words he needed to tell Cervanae of his father's plans. Then they came all at once, tumbling from his mouth in a torrent of emotion.

Cervanae listened closely and silently whilst Danial spoke of Shale Oil, the siting of a well, and the very real loss of her home.

She sighed deeply, "I had hoped this was at an end with your great uncle's passing."

Danial was flabbergasted. "You *knew* about this?"

She nodded, disappointment etched across her face. "Mr Harper-Fox – the elder – planned to make money from our beautiful land, destroying the ancient woodland. All for his own greed."

"And now it's my father's turn!"

"Do not judge him so harshly, Danial, son of Simon. Your father's heart *is* pure. He only tries to protect his family."

Guilt filled him, "But at *your* expense!"

"Many creatures call Frankly Woods their home. Creatures that he could not possibly hope to understand. It is these creatures – the different beings that dwell here – that make Frankly Woods magical."

For the briefest moment, Danial thought back to their previous meeting, then said, "Nature's magic!"

Cervanae smiled appreciatively. "There are many magical things in this world that do not contain *magic*. The sunrise on a frosty morn; a host of Starlings flying in beautiful formation; a spectacular sunset; the birth of new babies in the spring. All are magical, but without *magic*."

Danial wasn't sure he understood, but he was sure of how he felt about Cervanae, despite their brief time together.

"You're my only friend here – I don't want to lose you!" he cried.

"I am sure that is not true. You are a kind boy and must have many who enjoy your company."

"At home – my *old* home, yes; but not *here!*"

"Here you have your parents, and even your sister. Many would envy such a gift."

Danial had never thought of his family as a 'gift' before. "My parents hate me... and I hate my sister!"

"Hate is a strong and dangerous word. You should never *hate* anyone."

"Surely you feel that way about my father for destroying your home?"

"I hate no one."

"But where will you go?"

"It is not just my home, but home to many other creatures who dwell there," Cervanae replied, avoiding the question. "It is their birthplace, their native land. Frankly Woods date back to the earliest of pagan times and even before; they are as old as life itself."

"Dad says that nothing lives there except mice and rats."

"Your father is most wrong," Cervanae said with worry in her voice. "And many are already concerned. News travels swiftly whenever these ancient woodlands are in peril."

"Whispers on a breeze,
    swift, they soar like spears.
        Secrets both far and wide,
            news that brings sad tears."

The boy stared blankly.

Cervanae sighed. "You are young, Danial, son of Simon. Your innocence still protects you from life's harsh realities."

"What can we *do?*" Danial was now determined to stop his father's plans.

"We can *fight!*" she replied, passion in her voice.

"How?"

"We will find a way, together."

It was now Cervanae's turn to hug Danial back.

After a few moments, he looked around them, brushing white flakes from his head. The snow had now settled over half a metre deep around the darkened room.

"How is this happening?"

"Magic, of course."

"My mum doesn't believe in magic. She says I've been lying."

"You doubt your own senses?"

He shook his head.

"Nature has power, Danial. Nature *is* power. Men believe that they are its master, but in any battle nature always wins. But this time we must be swift."

Gulping hard, Danial stared at her blankly, nervous about what she meant.

"I don't understand."

"Our journey," she said, but the young boy was still none the wiser. "First however, I need to change."

"Change?!

"Close your eyes and count to ten."

Danial was no longer suspicious, but he *was* nervous. "Why?" he asked.

"Do you trust me?"

He nodded. Though fearful, he now obeyed her instructions. He closed his eyes and counted.

Chapter Ten

Danial reached a count of ten and opened his eyes and let out an astonished gasp.

A beautiful deer stood tall and proud before him. The beast was magnificent, with mighty antlers that would rival the most colossal stag, and hooves that were as shiny as if someone had just polished them. The deer bowed its head.

"It is I, Cervanae."

Danial's mouth dropped open, mind racing. He wondered whether he should turn and run... though quite how far he'd get on legs like jelly as they were now, he did not know.

"I— I—" he tried, but no other words came from his mouth. The sight of the giant deer so close to him was nothing less than intimidating.

The wondrous beast spoke again. "It is me, just a different 'version' than the one you know. I am still Cervanae, your friend."

"But... you're a *deer!*" Danial cried.

Cervanae responded, "I am many things, Danial, son of Simon: The ancient deer mother of old; the goddess-mother who flies through the shortest night. Legends of Santa Claus and his animal helpers flying across the sky are mere babes in my history. Since ancient times, it is I, the female reindeer, who flies my sleigh every midwinter. As the old year wanes, I stir all that sleeps to wake for the new."

"You're a *deer?*" Danial exclaimed, as if stuck on repeat.

Cervanae bowed her head, antlers brushing the snow-covered carpet.

"Yes, but I am also from the earth itself; I am Mother Christmas, created when man still believed in the natural wonders of the world. I carry the birds in the sky, the sun, the moon and even the stars with me; I journey through the darkness and bring life back with me."

"You're Father Christmas's' *wife?*"

Cervanae chuckled, her eyes full of devilment. "Not quite. You do not believe in Father Christmas though, do you?"

How did she know that?

Danial grew crimson. "Only little children believe in him. I'm older than that now"

"There is more magic in this world than you might think."

"Nature's magic again?"

The deer nodded. "If my current appearance truly makes you uncomfortable, I shall change back to the Cervanae that you know." She paused briefly, then continued, "However, my human form would find it difficult to achieve what I have planned next."

Danial felt anxious. What *was* planned next?

"I am still Cervanae, just a little different."

"A *little* different?" he huffed.

"*More* than a little then, I suppose," the beast laughed.

"C— Can I stroke you?" Danial asked nervously.

Cervanae lowered her head to him. "You may."

Danial moved tentatively closer and reached out a hand. The fur his fingers touched was thick yet soft, like velvet. He moved his hand up the animal's neck then gently brushed his hand along one of the gleaming antlers, which felt like bone, but was far smoother.

Suddenly, his trepidation disappeared and both of his arms reached out and hugged the deer tight.

"You see, I am still the same Cervanae, Danial, son of Simon."

"And you're still my friend?"

"We must be swift and go now. The day wanes rapidly and soon darkness will be upon us once more."

Danial shook his head. "*Go?* where?"

"Outside."

Cervanae's answer did not ease his concerns.

"My parents are already angry with me. If they find my room empty—"

"Do not fear," the deer reassured him, "as to your parents, all will appear the same."

"But the *snow?*" Danial looked doubtfully, eyeing the deep white drifts that now covered every surface.

"You can see these things only because I am here," Cervanae explained gently. "All will be as it was; there shall be no alarm."

Danial's worries eased slightly at her words. She had never lied to him yet, so he must believe her now.

"Now, take a firm grip of my antlers, swing aloft onto my back, and swift we shall we go."

Danial obeyed, hoisting himself up. He held onto the strong antlers as if his life depended on them... which it soon seemed it did, as with an explosive whoosh, they shot upwards through where the ceiling should have been, and towards the open sky.

Chapter Eleven

Whooping with delight as the rush of air hit him, Danial could not believe what was happening. He could see his house appear to shrink smaller and smaller the higher they flew.

"Hold on tight!" Cervanae cried. Another whoosh saw them speed even faster skywards, towards the now-huge moon that peeked out from behind a thick cloud. Danial felt as though they were so close he could touch it. He reached out a hand and was sure the man in the moon winked at him.

The excitement caused him to cry out in joy. He couldn't believe that he – Danial Harper – was here, on the back of a reindeer, riding this close to the moon; the same moon at which people had looked up and dreamed about since the dawn of time.

Cervanae flew across the icy sky, the duo illuminated by a halo of mist that surrounded the massive orb. "Do you see this beautiful moon, Danial, son of Simon?"

"Yes, of course."

"The deer mother flies through the night, bringing light to the aging year; it is a light brighter than the moon before us. She awakens those that sleep and helps them grow again. Some take longer than others; some are too comfortable in their beds and do not yet wish to wake. But Mother Nature will win once more, and all will return to vibrant life, however reluctant they may at first feel."

Deer and rider swooped back down, the wind howling around them as if they were on a the fastest rollercoaster. Soon Danial found himself above Frankly Village, where they hovered to watch as a large crowd heading towards the Green Man pub. The throng, so earnest in their conversations, did not even notice the soaring duo.

Danial sighed relieved; the sight of them above would surely have shocked anyone, and there would only have been more trouble if the fantastical news of a flying deer with a young boy as its rider was reported back to his parents.

Cervanae turned her head towards him, eyes thoughtful.

"Is there something you wish to see, Danial, son of Simon?"

His eyes grew wide.

"Ah," the deer nodded knowingly.

Danial's excitement grew as they made a quick turn, which first saw them fly fast over the Frankly Woods, the darkness of the trees a blessing to hide them from prying eyes below. From this angle, he could see how the woods stretched into the distance, way farther than he'd assumed.

To the north, he could just perceive the outlines of the Illusion Hills, with Black Tor reaching tall as if to try and touch the stars.

The sound of the rushing air began to quieten as they slowed until finally landing on top of a raised bank in near absolute silence.

"King Arthur's Burg," Cervanae stated with reverence.

Danial's heart pounded hard in his chest arriving at what he knew must be a magical place.

Cervanae indicated the area around them.

"It is said that on the darkest of nights, when there is no moonlight left in the sky, the legendary king and his Knights of Camelot can be seen at the ramparts of this ancient fortress, guarding it against those who may mean it harm."

The joy of seeing the Man in the Moon was replaced with Danial's expectation of an even greater sight.

From Cervanae came a shining orb, which rose high and brightly lit the landscape around them.

Danial slid off Cervanae's back and landed on soft snow, which crunched beneath his feet.

The burg was a slightly raised area that sat on top of a hill, surrounded by moderately steep banks and ditches; the undulations of the ground were barely visible under the blanket of white that now covered the land.

Danial spoke with disappointment in his voice, "It's just flat and snowy!"

Cervanae understood his despondency.

"Man has not dwelled in this place for a thousand years. All you see is what remains now, and time is a thief-snatcher. The burg was once truly magnificent and on cold winter nights, fires could be seen burning for miles from its elevated position. It was a beacon of hope and protection to all around."

"But, wouldn't such bright fires help any enemies?" Danial asked, somewhat confused.

The deer shook her head, trotting to the outer edge of the Burg. The boy followed.

"Look, even now you can see how its defences follow the natural contours of the hill. The ditches and banks are all that remains of what was a towering defensive wall. The ditches were some six metres deep; no attacking force could easily break through. Any foe foolish enough to try would soon be beaten back – or worse."

Cervanae grew pensive for a moment. "They were brutal days; days of warriors and clans. Long gone now, and best left to Father Time alone."

"What does *burg* mean?" Danial asked, the question having been rolling around his mind since he first saw the word on the old map.

"It means a fortified settlement or a walled hamlet."

"And is it true that there were actual knights living here?" Danial's fascination grew as he saw in his mind's eye visions of men both on horseback and standing, fighting skilfully with their swords.

Cervanae nodded.

"Brave warriors guarded this land; they guarded their king."

"King Arthur was *real?*" The boy gasped, his excitement now bubbling in his stomach.

"Legends that have been lost, found and retold throughout the mists of time tell tale of the warrior king known as Arthur," Cervanae continued, "and he was brave... but could also be foolhardy at times. The king took great risks to protect his people."

Danial's eyes grew as big as the moon.

"You *knew* him?" Danial spluttered.

The deer hummed her agreement, growing wistful.

"The fortification was larger than people imagine today. Outside the walls, an outer town stretched for miles, encircling the fortified buildings at its centre. When enemies attacked, the townsfolk would leave their homes and come to shelter within the burg's great walls," she explained with melancholy in her voice. "Life was hard then, but it was also a simpler time; a time when man respected the land and the seasons. All understood the power of nature and lived by its rules. But to most, those rules are long forgotten, the memory of them diminishing ever thinner as time ambles along its never-ending path. Man must not be allowed to destroy, yet it is in their nature. Do you understand, Danial, son of Simon?"

The young boy nodded, still trying to get his head around everything that he had just been told. Cervanae – who he believed yesterday to be a teenage girl – knew the legendary King Arthur... but that would make her over a thousand years old!

"Again, you doubt what you have learned, Danial, son of Simon." The deer looked at him but said no more on the matter. Instead she pointed and exclaimed, "Look yonder! The moon illuminates Frankly Woods. It is my ancient homeland and home to many friends."

"But for how long?" Danial stared sadly at the mass of blackness ahead.

"Your father is frightened for his family. He tries to rectify that fear through wrong choices. I cannot judge him for that!"

"*I* can!" Danial cried. "He can't destroy the woods! What would you do? Where would you go?"

"A meeting takes place on the morn amongst its inhabitants. We will agree on our plan of action then. Join us if you so wish."

Danial nodded his agreement.

"So you will come at dawn," Cervanae beckoned him to her, "but for now it grows late and we must head back."

Danial didn't *want* to go back. His anger had not abated, nor had his excitement. He wanted to explore some more, ride on the wind, feel its icy blast on his face... *anything* other than going back home and being called a liar.

Cervanae felt his hesitation. "You *must* return, Danial, son of Simon."

"But I want to stay with you!"

The deer shook its head. "I am your friend, but not your kin. A family sometimes may have happiness, sometimes it may have sadness, but it will always have love; this never stops. Your parents will soon discover that you do not lie, I am certain of this. Now scramble aboard – time waits for no man."

Danial knew well enough that she meant what she'd said and reluctantly obeyed. In an instant, they took off again, like a shooting star flashing across the heavens. The frigid wind whistled loudly around them, and in a matter of moments, Danial found himself back where they'd started – in his bedroom.

He slid off Cervanae's back and hesitantly looked around. There were no footprints in the carpet of snow. He smiled, relieved; his parents had not discovered his disappearance nor the unusual state of his room.

"We shall meet at dawn," Cervanae said as she bobbed her head in farewell.

Danial flung his arms around her neck, the soft velvet tickling him as he hugged her. "That was *ace!*"

Cervanae chuckled. "It was indeed. Now, you must close your eyes and count to ten once again. All will be as it was."

Trusting her entirely now, Danial obeyed.

When he opened his eyes, Cervanae had vanished; the snow had too, and both his bed and all the furniture were now visible, not covered in the soft, white blanket any longer.

Danial sighed disappointedly. He stared hard at the ceiling, wishing instead it would change back again.

Chapter Twelve

"It's *war!*" Mrs Briggs cried.

A loud chorus of approval followed her words.

Veronica Michaels, the young shopkeeper who was leading the meeting, tried and failed to calm the irate crowd sitting inside the pub. The place was packed to the rafters despite the inclement weather, Mrs Briggs's news having spread through the village like wildfire.

Never had there been such persistent snow like there was now; not in living memory. There were drifts over a metre deep in some places. Snow was piled up against every houses and building, hastily-scraped paths made for people on which to walk... or skid, which many did.

Yet people had come from far and wide to this hastily-arranged gathering... and they were not happy.

Thankfully for Danial, these people had been far to engrossed in their discussions to notice a flying deer – and with a young boy riding her, no less – swoop above their group as they had made towards the pub for the start of the meeting.

But would they have believed their eyes anyway? After all, most adults were too 'grown-up' to believe in magic.

Now an angry voice boomed over the already-raucous din in the Green Man.

"Fracking is *dangerous,*" Flynn Davies hissed. "They won't get away with it! They come and not only take over the hall, but try to ruin our village in the process! Well, I say never! Never! *Never!*"

In an attempt at bringing some calm to proceedings, Veronica Michaels coughed loudly and then addressed the assembled group.

"People, people! I have called this meeting today to discuss my findings with you," she said as the hubbub began to die down. "Since Mrs Briggs informed us of the new owners' plans, I have undertaken a great deal of research on the process involved, as you would expect. This includes what our legal rights are."

Silence had now descended and all eyes in the building were focused intently upon her.

Veronica continued, "A council *can* consider fracking bids from oil or gas companies to extract shale gas. The fracking itself occurs underground, using a process of wells, some almost three kilometres deep. The bidding company must submit their project for approval; it is then up to the council's planning committee whether to grant – or perhaps deny – permission."

"So, we badger the council?!" Shirley Abbott declared.

Veronica shook her head. "It's not just the council, but the government as well. The law has changed since the earlier days of this, allowing companies to frack *against* the wishes of the local community and any residents that it may affect."

"Scandalous!" A host irate of voices cried.

"They want to fast-track the process, without any need for public consultation before the *test* drilling goes ahead."

"Outrageous!" Doctor White cried aghast, "so we get no say in how we live?!"

"These changes, which had been oh-so-quietly put out for public consultation in the past, end a community's right to complain."

A roar of disapproval filled the pub.

"What does that mean for *us,* Veronica?" Arthur Abbott spoke above the disgruntled racket.

"In simple terms," she sighed, "our opinions will not be sought in the early stages of a new fracking site."

An audible gasp of horror grew ever louder.

"Oh, we'll have our say alright," Mrs Briggs snapped. "These people haven't dealt with the residents of Frankly Village before!"

Rousing cheers followed her words.

"I don't want to lose my job over this though," Old Joe, the gardener added with concern. "I can barely manage on my pension now. If I lost my wage..."

"So, the woods and village shall be destroyed for the sake of our *jobs*, Joe? Which would you choose, ultimately?" Mrs Briggs asked sternly.

The gardener looked sheepish but said no more on the matter.

"But, what can we *do?*" Shirley Abbott cried.

"Anything we have to," Veronica declared with determination. "My research shows that we are dealing with dangerous technology. Any successful contractor will start by pumping water into the ground to fracture it; there can be up to fifty thousand gallons of water at any one time. This can cause a significant reduction in our village's mains fresh water supply. And... what goes down must come up again! Contaminated fracking fluids can re-emerge, poisoning the water supply and even our rivers. When the dangerous water returns to the surface, methane gas can even be released polluting the very air that we breathe."

Horror-filled eyes stared at each other; Veronica carried on.

"Extra transport will be needed to bring materials in and to take the extracted gas out. Huge lorries will be thundering up and down our quiet country lanes, their fumes poisoning our children."

A loud chorus of boos followed, the loudest from Flynn Davies and his band of cronies. Everyone began to speak at once.

Shirley Abbott won the battle.

"My pub dates to the sixteenth century... all those lorries will bring the rafters down!"

"That's just the tip of the iceberg!" Veronica continued. "Fracking can affect the very ground that we stand on, causing earthquakes. If a test well is to be sited in Frankly Woods, as Mrs Briggs has relayed, the whole village will be at risk!.

"Our houses will topple!" Doctor White exclaimed.

Mrs Briggs shrieked, then blessed herself as if somehow that would help.

"So, echoing Shirley, *what* can we do to stop this?" her husband asked.

"We must deal with the new owners of Frankly Hall. *They* are the people who are allowing fracking to take place, permitting a test well to be sited on their land."

"I was so angry, I just walked out!" Mrs Briggs spat. "I am not going back, for fear that my tongue will run away from me!"

"You must!" Veronica said urgently.

"I will *not!*"

"We need someone at the house to report back. Verity can only help when term time ends, so will not have access to the hall until then. We *need* you."

"A spy?" Mrs Briggs's interest was raised.

"More of a... *detective,*" said Veronica, "to report on any new visitors to the hall. We need hard facts."

"I don't think I could be civil."

"You must, for the sake of our village and the woods," Doctor White said.

"We all played in there as children," Flynn Davies added gruffly. "My kids play there now!"

"Me, too!" Mrs Briggs returned to her youth.

"If *Detective Briggs* doesn't get the job done, what then?" Old Joe exclaimed doubtfully.

"We *fight!*" Veronica declared. "We stand up for our home, our health and our right to live in peace!"

Cheers followed her words.

"Will the Christmas fair still go ahead tomorrow?" Mr Asha, a new resident of the village, piped up from the crowd. His wife Safera smiled. She had made too much food to count.

"It certainly will!" Veronica spoke determinedly. "*Nothing* will stop our traditions."

"And the owners of the Hall?" Shirley Abbott asked.

"Frankly Villagers stand together, as they will soon discover to their cost!" Veronica declared.

The roar was back.

Chapter Thirteen

Danial's alarm clock shocked him awake.

He checked the time. It was five o'clock in the morning and still dark outside. Heavy curtains made his bedroom darker. He was not fond of getting up at such an ungodly hour.

Today was the Christmas fair and Cervanae had said to come to the woods at dawn. He wanted to leave early and be back in time for breakfast; anything to avoid another argument with his parents if they found his room empty.

Wearily, he climbed from his bed and looked out of his bedroom window. A freezing fog had started to descend, covering the land in a ghost-like haze. Breath visible before him, his sensible head wished that he could go back to bed. The *un*-sensible wanted to see Cervanae again, and to meet the friends that he'd heard so much about.

Dressing quickly – not just for the early morning meeting, but because the fire had died down and he was starting to shiver – Danial found his way out of the hall as fast as he could. He'd discovered a new trick – sliding down the banister – which helped enourmously.

It had stopped snowing, for the first time in days.

A frosty night had made the covering of white hard and slippy beneath his feet. Many times on his journey, he almost ended up on his backside. Thankfully though, he reached the woods quickly, despite the gloom.

Danial stood breathless at the threshold of the woods. Beyond, it looked spooky and not very inviting at all.

Rooted to his spot amongst the mist, his legs turned to jelly. A frightening realization filled his head.

He had no idea where Cervanae lived!

Danial racked his brain, trying to recall the old hollow where they had first met. To his horror, everything looked the same this morning in the snowy landscape. Summoning his last ounce of courage, he tentatively moved forward.

As he walked, every tree and branch looked the same as the last. Danial called out. Silence followed his words; only an icy wind whistled through the stark woodland. In the dull mist, the trees looked almost human-like, with branches for arms and a snow top for their heads. Ghostly figures. *Scary* figures.

Maybe this wasn't such a good idea after all.

How could he have been so stupid?

Danial shouted louder, the otherworldly trees not helping ease his fraught nerves. Deep despair filled him at the deafening silence that followed. He wanted to see his friend. The only friend he had here.

He *must* find Cervanae now...

The boy moved deeper into the thicket, careful to remember which direction he had come from, so as not to get lost again. It became harder and harder to see in the mist, which was even thicker now, enveloping everything it touched in its ghostly cape.

Danial trod cautiously. From experience, this snow-covered ground – which looked so innocent and fresh – held multiple dangers beneath its smooth-looking surface.

He was alone, truly alone. Danial hoped—

A noise to his side made him cry out. Wide eyes held dark orbs, which stared back at him intently.

The beautiful fox looked at him curiously, wondering if he was some kind of breakfast. Danial watched it in awe, its reddish-brown coat, and bushy tail magnificent against the stark white. Suddenly the fox fled, deciding that this wasn't an enticing meal after all. Danial knew he had to stop giving himself the heebie-jeebies...

He decided that he would call out again. If this did not work, he would make his way round into the village to find out if anyone there knew where Cervanae lived. The thought of meeting Freddy and Nathan Davies didn't appeal, but it was a risk worth taking if he could see his only friend. *Anything* was better than staying here alone with these stationary 'ghosts'.

Danial listened hopefully but was left disappointed, his shout not soliciting a response of any kind.

The village – and the Davies boys – it is, then.

Turning on his heel whilst summoning the courage to face his dreaded foes, Danial let out a gasp and almost jumped out of his skin.

Cervanae stood before him, her fur cape cascading down to the ground. She held a flaming torch in her hand, which seemed to create a magical halo of light around her.

"You came, Danial, son of Simon."

A wide smile spread across the boy's face. He hugged her to him. Immediately, the same comforting warmth as if he had just climbed into a warm bath coursed through his body. Words tumbled from his mouth.

"I couldn't find my way to the old hollow. I started to worry... about the ghosts!"

"Ghosts?" Cervanae looked confused. "It's the living that you must fear, not the dead. Never fear the elements. In the future, whenever you need me, repeat this verse...

Of bird, of horse, of Ox, of deer,
I call for Cervanae to appear here.
Be quick, be swift, come my way,
I need your help this very day."

Danial repeated the verse over and over, concentrating hard to get the words right. Finally, he had it down pat.

"What news do you bring?!" Cervanae asked.

"Not good."

The girl shook her head disappointedly. "Come, you shall meet my friends and inform us all."

Danial followed eagerly behind the flickering light, its flame whipping in the cold breeze. After a few minutes, he heard voices, quickening his step, anxious to see what lay past the dense thicket.

A large stag-head oak came into view, branches protruding like arms from its crown, centuries in the making. Beyond, he found himself in a secret grove.

Danial gasped at the spectacle that greeted them. An array of animals – some that he'd never even seen before – darted here and there over the snow-covered ground, all vying for a good spot.

"Greetings, Mother Christmas," A cow-like creature said as it approached.

Danial's mouth dropped open... *it could talk!*

"I see that you bring a young master."

He had never seen a cow like it. Apart from the astonishing fact that it could talk, its body was larger and more muscular than any normal cow you would see grazing in the fields. He stuttered, mouth agape, "Y— you can speak?"

"Of course!"

The creature eyed him, seemingly perturbed by the question as if a talking animal was an everyday occurrence.

"I've never seen a cow that talks," Danial said, his face still agog.

The creature looked aghast. "Cow? I am an *Ox!*"

"Do not be offended Aurochs," Cervanae said, placating the irked beast. "Danial is from the land of men and is not yet familiar with the wonders of nature. He means no disrespect."

The ox huffed haughtily.

"The young master is welcome, Mother Christmas, even if from the land of men."

Danial had stopped listening, his eyes beholding the other talking creatures around them. Foxes chatted with deer, rabbits with badgers. The thing that astonished him most was the sight of a magnificent black steed, deep in conversation with a pair of Robin Redbreasts perched on top of its back.

He closed his eyes tightly, not quite believing what he was seeing. They grew ever wider as he reopened them. The strange trio were still chatting away.

Cervanae moved towards the great stallion, which towered above them both.

"Come Danial, meet Tarpan."

He hesitantly followed, ice crunching with every step. The size of the beast astonished him. It was at least double the size of any normal horse.

"Lady of the Forest, greetings!"

The charger bowed its head. Wings fluttered wildly; a cacophony of angry protests followed.

"Forgive me, dear friends!" Tarpan exclaimed. "In the briefest moment of silence, I thought that you were no longer with me!"

The affronted robins chirped and flew away to an overhanging branch; the noise they made even louder than before.

Tarpan whinnied, winking at Danial.

"Deep thanks for rescuing me My Lady, Young Master. Robin Redbreasts make *such* a racket; I can barely hear myself think."

Danial nodded silently, astonished by this talking horse. He pondered Tarpan's words, 'Lady of the Forest'. Cervanae had mentioned 'Mother Christmas' before, but now he was even more unsure as to who she really was.

His thought was snatched away by the words she spoke next.

"How finds the steed of the fairies?"

The boy could not believe what he was hearing. The word blurted from his mouth. *"Fairies?"*

"They have many names," Cervanae answered. "Pixies, Brownies, Elves, Gnomes, Fays. We call them *Greenies* as it is easy to remember them that way."

"The Spirits of the Forest shall arrive at any moment," the steed continued, "and there will be such a rumpus – such a commotion – that even the Robin Redbreasts will seem quiet by comparison."

Danial looked dumbfounded. It had been a strange morning thus far, with talking animals, and now fairies to boot. A long, deep sigh escaped him. He was convinced that he would wake up at any moment, only to find out that this whole thing had been a dream.

"Stand well back!"

Cervanae's words interrupted his musings.

Ahead, a small dot of light appeared, growing bigger and bigger like someone was blowing up bubble gum until it was fit to burst...

...and then it did!

A magical explosion ensued; a thousand fireflies flew here, there and everywhere, like a giant swarm of buzzing bees. Danial looked closer; the explosion was not fireflies at all, but tiny winged creatures.

The swarm erupted into a chorus of noise and excitement.

"Welcome, Spirits of Midwinter, Greenies, on this pressing morn," Cervanae said majestically as she bowed her head.

"Greencoates!" Aurochs said in unison with them, affronted at the use of the apparently wrong name.

Cervanae raised her eyes exasperated.

Two tiny creatures, dressed in the most spectacular costumes, approached.

"Danial, may I introduce Mab and Oberon, King and Queen of the Greencoates." She muttered under her breath. *"Or Greenies..."*

The two fairies smiled, "Welcome, young master."

Danial was flabbergasted. Both creatures stood no more than two inches tall; each was dressed in fine gold and silver robes. Delicate silk capes floated around them, almost like ghosts floating in the icy breeze.

He nervously held out his little finger to shake each tiny hand. "Pleased to meet you."

A mass of giggles filled the air around them, the fairy folk as astonished to see a boy as Danial was to see them. They crowded around him for a better look, giggles soon becoming a tumult of excited chatter.

"Enough!" Aurochs chided. "Where is your guardian hiding?"

He looked around them glumly. The Greenies tittered amongst themselves as behind him a small sapling suddenly sprang to life. Danial stared agape as the tree began to move of its own free will.

It stepped towards the ox, growing ever bigger as it did, resting a branch on top of his back. Aurochs jumped, much to the Greenies' mirth.

"I see that you have finally crawled from shadow," the ox hissed with annoyance, not enjoying being the butt of the joke.

"Good morning, Spriggan," Cervanae bobbed her head.

The tree nodded back. "Lady of the Forest, I see that you bring a young visitor – Danial, son of man."

Though he wanted to, Danial could not speak. *How did it know his name? And what did 'of man' mean?*

"It is a rare sight for a human to see a Spriggan, Danial, unless of course, that human has angered her by its actions towards the fairy-folk." Cervanae gestured to the tree. "Behold, may I introduce the ancient tree spirit, watcher of the fairies, nature's guardian. She metes out punishment to those who dare harm the 'otherworld'."

"My father?" Danial asked, concerned.

His alarm grew as the tree stepped towards him, changing shape before his eyes. The leaves morphed into the face of a wizened old man before suddenly disappearing.

Danial stiffened at its made its way back to his side. The Spriggan sniffed him.

"Yes, *son of man*... you can smell the poison!"

He was not sure what it meant by 'poison', but the other animals around him appeared to understand fully. For a moment, he did not feel welcome at all.

"Danial is friend not foe, ancient Spriggan," Cervanae chided.

"He is a *human*, nature's destroyer!" the tree hissed before disappearing again on the wind.

"As you may gather, humans are not her favourite beings," Cervanae tried to reassure the boy. "She sees only the destruction and damage that they cause. As guardian of the fairy kingdom, you are her enemy. Do you understand?"

Danial nodded, grateful still to have one friend, at least.

"It is time to begin," Aurochs announced, tutting scornfully at the continued delay. "What news from the land of men?"

"John has not arrived," Tarpan said.

The ox snorted, *"Him!"*

"John?" Danial cried. "Another boy, like me?"

"Of sorts," Cervanae smiled, "but as old as time itself."

Danial looked confused.

"*Nature's* boy," Tarpan added helpfully.

"Nature's *pest!*" Aurochs spat.

"Aurochs thinks John feral," the steed explained.

Danial's brow furrowed; he'd heard that word said by a villager.

"It means *untamed*, Danial, son of Simon," Cervanae answered his question. "He is called the Wild Man of The Woods.

The boy nodded, finally understanding what Tarpan had meant.

"Wild *Thug* of The Woods is more apt," Aurochs hissed in contempt.

"Ah, he arrives; John Barleycorn."

Danial looked eagerly around for the other boy but could not see him. He followed Cervanae's gaze, which now rested on the stag-head oak. He rubbed his eyes, taking in the gleam of bright light that had suddenly appeared on a blade of grass beneath it.

The ray disappeared a second later, replaced by a small head protruding out from the ancient bark. Danial stumbled back shocked. The head was joined by arms and legs, and soon a young man, aged no older than eighteen years, stood before them. Whether a boy or a man, he could not answer for sure.

For the briefest moment, John did not move. Then he sprang here, there and everywhere, like a jack-in-the-box, jumping madly around, whooping with joy and excitement as he did. He landed on the ox's back and Aurochs kicked out, bucking his legs; the wild figure flew off his back and was thrown high into the air. Laughing all the way he fell into a crumpled heap on the ground, before springing to his feet and brushing himself down.

For the first time, Danial got a proper look at this John Barleycorn boy.

Dressed from head to foot in green, his face was completely covered with leaves; he was no boy that Danial had ever seen before. Branches and vines sprouted from his face, with red autumn berries dotted around like jewels, each adorning the greenery.

The strange creature stood no taller than himself, and had a mischievous grin firmly fixed on his face. He bowed a greeting to Cervanae, his oh-so-pale blue eyes holding her own.

"You are late, John Barleycorn," Cervanae scolded.

"But always worth the wait, Mother Christmas," he replied gleefully.

Aurochs snorted, addressing the assembled creatures, and ignoring the fantastical youth.

"Welcome, nature spirits, dear friends; finally we shall begin." He moved to the centre of the secret grove and continued, more than a little condescendingly. "We are summoned here on a grave matter; a matter that shall affect us all. We had hoped that this had all ended, with the passing of the last human 'owner' of these woods. However, it seems that we were wrong. Mother Christmas has informed us of the new owner's plans; the news will not cheer you."

Danial's attention left the ox for a moment due to the arrival of John Barleycorn at his side. He looked him up and down.

"So, you are a boy? You resemble me, but I am more handsome. Wherever are your leaves?"

"Quiet!" Aurochs hissed, his disapproval glaringly obvious.

John Barleycorn smirked but said no more.

Aurochs nodded to Cervanae.

She turned to Danial. "Please, tell us what news you bring."

All eyes fell upon him. The young boy hesitated.

A comforting hand was placed on his shoulder. Cervanae smiled, "Do not fear, I am here."

Danial sighed, somewhat reassured. He began to relay the conversation that had taken place with his father about fracking.

Around him, there was only silence. The clatter and commotion from earlier had disappeared on the wind.

Danial pulled a leaflet out of his coat pocket and read the title out loud, 'The Benefits of Fracking: A New Age in Energy'. After composing himself, he proceeded to read its entire contents.

When he had finished, Aurochs raised his eyes. "*The Benefits of Fracking? All for our good and wellbeing?* Balderdash!"

"Man cannot see the beauty around him," Cervanae cried. "Modern-day life steals away the old ways."

John Barleycorn piped up, "Modern-day *greed* would be more apt!"

Aurochs' eyes grew wide.

"For once, John Barleycorn, we agree on something. Man's greed alone will destroy Frankly Woods."

"They must be made to see the magic of this place, how sacred it is," Tarpan contributed.

"But *how?*" Oberon enquired gravely. "Their old ways are long gone. How do we get them back, how do we get them to understand?"

"We'll find a way," Danial cried, *"together!"*

For a moment those assembled looked doubtful that a human was prepared to help them. Disbelieving chatter took place.

It ended when Mother Christmas took Danial's hand.

"Let battle commence!"

An explosion of cheers followed, the scene erupting like a volcano.

"So, you are definitely committed to helping us?" Cervanae asked as she accompanied Danial back to the edge of the woodland.

"I am."

She looked around them. "You must be swift. When the East Wind blows, we shall have cold."

"I thought it was the North Wind?"

"The North brings *snow*, but the East brings *cold*. Snow and ice are never a good combination."

"I don't feel that cold," Danial noted.

"My old magic protects you." Cervanae raised her hand above him and muttered an incantation. The warmth Danial had felt earlier now increased tenfold. "You must go. Time, tide and a Christmas fair wait for no man."

Danial smiled. He made to move but then stopped.

"May I ask you something?"

Cervanae nodded.

"They called you Mother Christmas but also the Lady of The Forest. What is your true name?"

"I am many things, Danial, son of Simon," She smiled. "Mother Christmas, Lady of the Forest, Great Mother Goddess, Deer Mother of Old... I even have a feast day."

"A *what?*" Danial replied.

"People honour me across many lands, especially in the north."

"But *why?*"

Her eyes grew narrow.

"I mean... aren't you're just a girl and me just a boy? I don't underst—" Danial stammered, worried that he had upset his only friend.

"I am not offended," Cervanae reassured him. She continued wistfully. "It is complicated, Danial, son of Simon. I date from pagan times – long ago, when man lived by the seasons. Modern technology has taken him into towns and cities. He has forgotten the old lore."

Danial sighed. His father was the main culprit in all of this.

"We need to show the humans nature's *real* value, it's worth – a gift to be cherished, not destroyed."

Danial nodded. He turned to walk away.

"Which day is your feast day?"

"The winter solstice, December 21st."

"Can I come and see you then?"

"Just look out of your bedroom window on that darkest night. The Deer Mother will fly across the starry skies, her reindeer leading the way."

"Like... Father Christmas?"

Cervanae chuckled, "Just like old St Nicholas himself."

Chapter Fourteen

The 12th of December had started with a mad rush.

Danial had managed to sneak back into his bedroom without being seen, though he was certain that he'd left a trail of mud on the stairs. He'd quickly changed back into his pyjamas and kicked his clothes under the bed; everything was as it had been.

Ella came to wake him at eight o'clock for breakfast.

"We'll have no sulking today," she stated. "Up for breakfast, come on. We have a busy day ahead."

"So you want to eat with a liar, then?"

"I want to eat with my son, and have a nice day together. It's Christmas, the season to be joyful, the season for family." She came over and kissed the top of his head. "Your breakfast is on the table."

His mum left the room.

Danial could not argue with her words. Christmas was the season for family, even if *his* family were a pain. Regardless, he loved them all – even Lily when she was not screeching. He climbed out of bed and yawned loudly. It had already been a very long day.

The boy dressed quickly, brushing down his dirty clothes from under the bed to hide any tell-tale signs, and was down for breakfast in a trice. A large helping of scrambled eggs, bacon, three sausages and toast followed. Danial began to wolf them down.

"You seem hungry," Simon laughed.

The boy nodded. After not eating properly for nearly a day, he would have eaten anything put in front of him.

He helped himself to seconds, but was stopped from getting a third helping – much to his annoyance, as his mum didn't want him to be sick.

Breakfast over, they all began to get ready for the Christmas Fair.

A brisk walk was planned to 'brush off the cobwebs' as Simon had said. The heavy mist from earlier had begun to lift, the sun now partially visible in the clearing haze. Cold still gnawed at Danial's bones, despite being wrapped up like an Eskimo by Ella.

The walk from Frankly Hall to the village was pleasant. Danial had to admit that city life was no comparison; the beautiful countryside that surrounded their new home had no city comparison. There was so much to explore here, so many things he didn't yet know about. How long would it remain this beautiful if his father had his way?

Danial couldn't stop his anger from growing again, bubbling up inside like a boiling kettle. He remembered his mother's words, 'I want to spend a nice day with my son'.

He had to help Cervanae, and stop his father's plans, but knew he'd struggle to get the chance today.

They reached Frankly Village.

On their approach they saw a long queue of people lined up outside the village hall for the Christmas fair. At precisely eleven o'clock the doors opened and the assembled throng crowded into the building. A wonderful festive sight greeted the family as it was their turn to enter. Different stalls laden with gifts, food and sparkling festive decorations filled the hall, shining like the brightest of stars.

In a far corner of the large room, a small pile of freshly cut Christmas trees sat, the heady smell of pine wafting over them. Beyond was a small grotto, with Father Christmas himself waiting to give out presents to the line of children who had already joined the queue. Underneath the white beard however, Arthur Abbott's distinct features could be seen.

There were plenty more villagers helping out.

Veronica Michaels served behind a local produce food stall, helped by her sister Verity. A lovely aroma of fresh mince pies pleased all who passed by. Shirley Abbott stood behind a stall that was serving mulled wine. Safera's spices wafted lovely smells from the east, accompanying exotic foods on her display, and Flynn Davies's table was crammed full of meat and home-grown vegetables. Besides him stood his two boys, Freddy and Nathan, on their best behaviour for once.

Mrs Briggs had nominated herself as 'overseer', floating from stall to stall like the Queen. She nodded her approval, much to the amusement (and sometimes annoyance) of the various stallholders gathered. It had only been a day since the devastating news had broken in the village, but she had already managed to worm her way back in as housekeeper at Frankly Hall. Although Ella had proven difficult to convince at first, Mrs Briggs had soon won her around.

The old woman relished her role of spy, taking to it with gusto. She enjoyed the intrigue, her importance to the cause, and a part of her hoped it wouldn't end. For the first time in years she felt useful again, putting on the best acting performance of her life – so much so that the owners of Frankly Hall were still none the wiser that the whole village now knew of their plans.

A lot of important work had been done since they'd found out. The main force, Veronica, kept them all informed with the latest news. She'd become head of the opposition.

It was a fight that they were going to *win!*

A buzz of excitement filled the hall; laughter mingled with children's excited cries. The mood was so positive that at first, the Harper family's arrival went unnoticed.

Sadly, that didn't last too long.

The excited buzz soon died down into a disgruntled mutter, soon followed by a deathly silence.

"Good morning," Simon smiled.

There was no reply. He shrugged and headed towards a stall that contained old railway carriages with Danial; Ella and Lily went the other way.

"Look, Danial! I used to play with these when I was a child," Simon beamed, holding up a Hornby engine. Immediately, he was transported back to his youth. His eyes then fell on a Hornby Dublo *Mobil Gas* oil train, still in its original box. A favourite childhood toy that he had not seen for years. "How much?" he asked.

Doctor White glanced at Veronica who shook her head, a frown fixed firmly on her face.

"Sorry, it's sold," he muttered, clearly uncomfortable and not willing to meet Simon's eye.

"Can I have this, Dad?" Danial spotted a Hornby R722 *KitKat* van.

"Do you have enough pocket money left for it?"

The boy nodded, reaching into his coat pocket.

"That's not for sale either," Doctor White continued. "Everything has been sold or is reserved. I have nothing to sell to you."

Danial looked disappointed.

At the other end of the hall, Ella and Lily reached the cake stall. She sniffed at the aroma of hot mince pies which now filled her nostrils. "Such a beautiful display! Shall we buy some cakes, Lily?"

The young girl nodded. Her attention was soon caught by the grotto and Father Christmas. Lily ran over to join the queue of children.

"Everything is sold," Veronica said sharply. Verity turned away, busying herself with some invisible task. Ella took in the laden stall, heaving with produce.

"Everything?" Ella asked surprised.

Veronica nodded; the frown was not budging.

Disappointed, Ella walked over to join Lily. She was just about to hand over the two-pound charge when Stan Smith, dressed as an elf, stopped her in her tracks.

"Sorry, the grotto is closed."

Ella's gaze fell onto the other children.

Stan continued firmly, "They've already paid and will be able to see Father Christmas. You've arrived late, so your child cannot."

"The hall has only been open for ten minutes."

"You're too late!" Stan persisted. "Go, you're not welcome here."

"Not welcome?" Ella looked confused.

Tears filled Lily's eyes. She gasped between sobs. "I... can't see... Father... Christmas?"

Ella comforted her. Simon and Danial joined them. "We're too late for the grotto," she said.

Simon looked at his watch, "But it's eleven fifteen."

"I couldn't buy any cakes either."

Simon looked perplexed. "We couldn't buy any trains. They'd all 'sold out'."

"We're not welcome here." Ella eyed Stan, who quickly ushered another child in to meet Father Christmas. "Can't you see what's going on? I *told* you she was listening!"

"She?"

"Mrs Briggs... the fracking!"

Simon shifted uncomfortably, trying to shush Ella.

"They *know*, Simon!" she continued. "All the cakes and trains are sold. We're too late for the grotto, we're not welcome..."

The penny finally dropped. Simon looked at Ella, distraught. "They know!"

Ella nodded. It was as if a big spotlight had suddenly lit them up. A whole hall of unfriendly faces were staring at theirs. Rage engulfed Ella. The villagers knew of their plans, but they were punishing her *children*... and no one did that!

She spoke loudly. "I find it petty that grown adults should take their grievances out on a six-year-old child. I hope that you're all proud of yourselves?"

Veronica Michaels walked haughtily towards them.

"How *dare* you judge us when it's *you* who are trying to destroy our beautiful village. Do you think that we will let you ruin this place with dangerous technology?"

Mrs Briggs ducked quickly out of sight with Old Joe, choosing to watch from the shadows.

"So, you agree you're punishing an innocent child?" Ella continued.

Veronica shook her head, "It is you alone who punish your daughter, not us. *We're* not selling Frankly Woods to a fracking company for greed alone!"

"When did you find out?" Simon cried exasperated.

"We have taken steps to stop your plans," Veronica continued as if he had not asked the question.

"Why didn't you talk to us about this before?" Ella cried, aggrieved. "This unpleasantness is completely unnecessary."

"And give you the chance to justify your actions?" Shirley Abbott replied as he joined Veronica.

"My pub dates back to the sixteenth century. There would be trucks rumbling past at all hours, shaking its rafters to the core. And *that's* just for starters..."

"But fracking is *safe!*" Simon interrupted. "I have some leaflets for you all, so you can see the benefits."

A loud murmur of discontent followed his words.

"The only *benefit* is that you'll fill your pockets," Doctor White added as he joined the fray. "You in the big house, surrounded by land; Frankly Woods skirts the *village*. Fracking won't hurt you, but it will *us.*"

"That is unfair!" Ella said, emotionally. "Like you all, I truly believed that fracking was unsafe. But after reading the information, I have been convinced."

"How many pounds did it take to 'convince' you?" Shirley Abbott spat.

Ella looked at her husband and said, "We need to go; this is upsetting the children."

"Your children are not the only ones who matter," Veronica continued. "What will happen when *our* children get ill from drinking polluted water? Where will *they* live when an earthquake brings their houses down?"

"You're being ridiculous now," Simon said sternly.

"We're leaving," stated his wife.

Ella took Lily's hand and moved towards the door. Simon followed quickly with Danial.

"Yes, you *will* leave," Veronica shouted behind them. "You are banned from the village. Banned from the *school!*"

Ella could not reply, desperately trying to hold back tears that threatened to fall. Once outside, they flowed freely.

Simon hugged her close to him. "Everything will be alright. We'll sort it."

Danial joined his father. Despite the anger he felt towards his parents, he didn't want to see his mother cry, ever.

"This is *not* what I had hoped for," Ella sobbed as she wiped tears away. "This was supposed to be a new life, a new chance for us... but now we're barred from the village, even the school. The kids are supposed to start there in January!"

"I promise, it will all be sorted," Simon assured her.

"I told you, Dad," Danial piped up. "People will lose their homes."

"Not *this* again!" Simon snapped. "For the last time, nobody lives in Frankly Woods!"

Chapter Fifteen

The phone call that they'd been dreading finally came.

Steve Wyatt raised his eyes at the panicked voice on the other end of the line. "Slow down man, breathe."

Wyatt placed the phone onto speaker so his boss Henry Carney could listen to the tumult that followed.

They heard it all as Simon ranted.

The villagers knew all their plans, the family was barred from the village and school, his wife and children were upset, and he'd had second thoughts about the fracking happening at all...

Henry Carney spoke after listening for a good five minutes.

"Do not *worry*, Mr Harper."

"Don't worry?" Simon sounded like he had been breathing in helium, his voice was so high.

"Do you believe in the *sustainability* of fracking?" Henry continued calmly.

"Yes... but I also want my family to be happy, Mr Carney," Simon replied.

"Of course you're anxious, Mr Harper," Wyatt interrupted.

"*Anxious* is the understatement of the year!"

"We've come across this problem countless times," the Texan continued. "A town finds out about our plans, then all hell breaks loose. The *doomsters* go around stating it's the end of the world if we frack; it's ridiculous. Fracking is a clean fuel process that will ease our reliance on fossil fuels. They just don't understand the *process.*"

"How do we *get* them to understand?" Simon replied, only slightly calmer than before.

Henry Carney spoke steadily, "We *educate* them."

"That's all well and good Mr Carney, but you have not met these villagers. I don't think *educating* them would help."

"There will always be obstacles to change, Mr Harper."

"But the changes are affecting *us,* not you, Mr Carney. I do agree we need to talk to them, but one-to-one. Show them the same leaflet that you gave to me. The leaflet explains fracking and its benefits. How can they think that I would put my family at risk?"

Steve Wyatt shook his head, eyes panicked. He'd do anything to avoid a one-to-one between Harper and any of the villagers. It had happened before, their plans ruined by interfering busybodies chucking their toys out of the pram.

He would *not* let it happen again, especially as he'd already spent the big bonus that he was going to receive. They'd simply put the pressure on, piling it sky-high until their prey was forced to change their mind. A bunch of country yokels would never beat him...

"Mr Harper, I don't think that is a very good idea and I'd advise strongly against talking one-to-one with anyone. Leave *us* to deal with it. We are in London on business at present but will be back in a few days. We have a contact in the House of Lords who will clear our path. The law has now changed, allowing companies to frack *against* the wishes of a local community. The villagers of Frankly can do nothing. It's *your* land and *you're* free to do what you want with it."

"The House of Lords?" Simon exclaimed, shocked. "Who?"

"Sir George Balkour."

"I've never heard of him!"

"He knows many influential people; people who will get things done. This passage can be as smooth as you want it to be," Wyatt continued on a roll. "Please don't concern yourselves over the villagers, *especially* after the way they have treated you all. We will handle this."

Simon was not convinced. "But wouldn't it be easier to t—"

"Please Mr Harper," Carney joined the conversation once again. "I *promise* that we will protect your family; we'll win the village around. In the next few days, we will drop the leaflets; we'll show how fracking is good for the community and show how *they* will prosper just as much a you will."

Simon was silent.

"For gods' sake!" Wyatt snapped, irritation oozing from every pore. "We even have to minimize the release of any gases as a condition of our license from the Department of Energy and Climate Change. It's all *regulated*, all *checked*. If we fail at any stage to do our job properly, we're not allowed to frack at all."

"But..."

"Steve is right, Mr Harper." Henry Carney stepped in again. "*We* will deal with Frankly Village and its residents, smooth the path so that you don't have to."

"I don't *ever* want to see my wife or children cry again!"

"All will be well. We promise!"

Chapter Sixteen

George Balkour did not like being summoned.

He entered the lift gruffly, his eyes practically on stalks watching out for any press that might have followed him. You can never be too careful...

Paranoia and panic remained with him as he took the lift to the fifth floor. The door opened and he checked that the coast was clear. Furtively, he made his way along the corridor towards the back stairs, sliding through the emergency exit there.

Balkour made his way down to the third floor, the floor that he had been called to for 'talks'. He hated confrontation and was not looking forward to the meeting that was about to take place.

These Americans are so...

His thought was snatched away as he reached room 321. He knocked.

Steve Wyatt's acerbic tone greeted him, "You're late!"

Balkour checked his watch. "Only thirty minutes; traffic was bad. This *is* London after all!"

He did not like being told off. As a lord he was used to being the one giving orders and having people jump to them. This was a new sensation that he didn't like or appreciate at all. He glared at Wyatt.

"What news?" Henry Carney's Texan drawl filled the hotel room.

The glare disappeared in an instant; he was talking to the organ grinder, not the monkey.

"Wonderful view," Balkour commented as he sat down beside Carney on a luxurious sofa that would not have looked out of place in Buckingham Palace. Outside, the River Thames shone in the bright autumn sunshine, framing the snowy city streets beyond. He could get used to this... and would do anything to have a view like it.

Like most landed gentry, he'd lately fallen on hard times. It did not help that his extravagant lifestyle far outweighed his earnings. And he did *not* want to be the lord who lost everything, the failure who let the cards fall. Reluctant though he was to admit it, he needed Shale Oil as much as they needed him. He had to be here whether he liked it or not...

"You're not here for the view!" Wyatt snapped.

Balkour's glare returned. This American was so *rude!* Didn't he know who he was talking to? A peer of the realm!

"Things are progressing," Balkour responded, ignoring the dig. This *colonial* didn't understand the importance of history, viewing the world from the perspective of his trailer park

"How so?" Carney asked.

"I have placed people in the various departments to pile on the pressure. Smooth our path."

"*Which* departments?" Carney pressed.

"The Oil and Gas Authority, the Department of Energy and Climate Change, Health and Safety Executive, and the Environmental Agency. It is all moving along nicely, don't worry."

"While my money is on the line, Balkour," Carney responded tartly, "I'll worry!"

Balkour laughed, but his mirth was met by a deathly silence, Carney and Wyatt not seeing the joke. This was a tough crowd...

"And the Lords?" Wyatt sat down opposite them, pouring his boss and himself a glass of whisky.

"None for me?" the peer enquired hopefully.

"We haven't heard anything from you that would *warrant* a celebration drink!" Wyatt spat.

"The *Lords?*" Carney's drawl interrupted.

Balkour sighed and sat back in his seat. "You will always have the anti-fracking brigade predicting the end of the world, or the extinction of this species or that tree if we frack. I have plenty on side in the House, and just as many waiting on the sidelines. They just need a *little* more incentive to see things exactly as we do."

He looked at Carney hopefully.

"You've had all the money you're going to get from me," the Texan affirmed as he took a slug from his glass. "Any *incentive* will have to come from what's already been advanced to you."

Balkour looked aghast. He had nothing to give; his advance was already gone. He was a Lord and lived a certain way; didn't they understand that?

Wyatt's next words answered his question.

"Don't mess with us Balkour, you won't win. You would not want us as an enemy."

Balkour gulped hard. There was definitely a threat in those words.

"Just do your job," Carney added, a scowl firmly fixed on his face. "Get this through, I want no hiccups. Earn your keep!"

Chapter Seventeen

The day had begun quietly. The family sat down to a breakfast prepared by Mrs Briggs. Ella thought that she seemed quieter than usual, which was no surprise after the horror at the fair a few days previous. She had not said one word about the whole thing, as if she was up to something.

Ella pushed the thought away. Maybe she was becoming paranoid. But who could blame her? She had barely gotten a wink of sleep since the awful experience. The nightmare repeated over and over in her head; she kept hearing the words telling her that their family were barred from the village and the school...

How had it come to this?

Simon escaped to his office after breakfast to avoid the usual argument that took place each morning now between wife and son. Danial wanted to go out and explore, but Ella thought it was too cold and wanted him to stay indoors.

Their quarrel could still be heard reverberating around the lofty halls ten minutes later, this time joined by something unfamiliar. Simon strained his ears to listen to a distant hum, but could not fathom it out. The hum increased with each passing moment. Soon Ella burst into the room.

"People!"

Simon stared none the wiser.

"Coming up the drive... with placards!" Ella stuttered.

What *was* she on about?

Ella pointed out of the window, her face pale as if she'd seen a ghost. The din grew louder. Simon jumped to his feet. He rushed to join her, becoming open-mouthed at the sight that greeted them.

A crowd of people was walking up the drive towards the hall. Shouts and chants could be heard amongst the placard-waving mass.

"Fracking no, traitors go!"

"My God!" Ella gasped, becoming even paler.

"What's going on?" Danial asked as he joined them.

Ella grabbed her husband. "I'm calling the police!"

"I don't think we're at that stage *quite* yet," Simon smiled reassuringly. "Everything will be fine, please don't worry!"

Worry was an understatement...

Simon left his office, Ella running after him.

"Stay here!" She shouted to her son. Though only small and slight, nobody would hurt her family while she had breath left in her body.

The hall door creaked open, almost groaning in anticipation of what was to come. The chants grew louder and for the first time Simon could make out clearly what was written on the placards.

'Fracking stop or family rot!' was one choice slogan, along with *'Our children matter too!'*, and *'Stop now or trouble we vow!'*.

For a brief moment fury erupted inside Simon. How *dare* these people threaten his family? Ella peered over his shoulder at the throng, who seemed to become more hostile with each passing moment. She herself now saw the placards and gulped hard.

"I'm calling the police, now!"

Simon shook his head. "No. Let me talk to them; there's been enough trouble already."

"They don't look ready to talk," Ella cried, "they look as if they want to string you up!"

"Please, stop!" Simon shouted as he stepped out of the hall, appearing far braver than he felt. "There is no need for any of this."

Protesting voices boomed from the bottom of the stone steps. The group swelled, growing even more irate at his presence.

"Traitors!"

"You're on private property," Simon shouted above the din. "You're scaring my family. If you don't leave, we will have to call the police."

The hostile ruckus exploded again.

"What about our families?" Shirley Abbott shouted. "Should we sit back and let you ruin our village, our children's futures?"

Simon shook his head.

"You're mistaken, fracking is a clean source of energy. I'll fetch some leaflets so you can read about it."

"We've read all that we need to know!" Veronica Michaels spat. "Frankly Woods – an ancient woodland – will be destroyed, .and all for you to make money."

"Fracking will benefit us *all*. There will be help for the village too."

A howl of laughter followed his words.

The noisy chanting started again.

"I have spoken with Mr Carney, the owner of Shale Oil, the company who wishes to frack. We have decided to arrange a meeting in the village hall on December 22nd, if you'll allow it. That will give us both time to prepare our arguments, and we can discuss things properly then. Everyone will have a say and we can explain how fracking will help us all."

"It'll be a very short meeting," Doctor White cried, "there are NO benefits to this terrible technology."

"You're wrong!" Simon continued unabashedly. "We can arrange the meeting for seven o'clock that evening, so as many people as possible can attend." Simon looked around them. "If you agree?"

Veronica nodded, attempting to placate the rowdy crowd. She failed. A small mob of troublemakers at the back, led by Flynn Davies, roared their anger. A rock flew up through the air, smashing a window.

"I'm calling the police, now!" Ella shouted, reaching for her mobile phone. Danial and Lily joined her on top of the steps.

"Stop!" Veronica roared at the crowd. Her eyes fell onto the children, who gripped their mother tightly. "We're victims here, don't make us the guilty ones."

She looked around at the assembled horde, who had quietened down at the appearance of the youngsters.

"We're not here to frighten children; they're not the enemy. You'll all have your say at the meeting."

"As long as we do," came Flynn Davies's gruff voice above the crowd. Veronica glared at Flynn and his cohorts.

"Please don't call the police, there will be no more trouble I promise," said Veronica. "I do apologise for the window. Send me the bill for its repair and the church fund will pay."

Simon stopped his wife.

"I will arrange the meeting as soon as you leave," Simon said. "But rest assured, no one will threaten my family!"

"Just as it should be." Veronica agreed. "I hope you heed your words with regards to *our* children too?"

Chapter Eighteen

Simon Harper's words did not go down well.

Steve Wyatt grew exasperated but tried to control his growing annoyance. Why didn't these Brits *listen?*

"There was no *need* for you to do that, Mr Harper. We said that we would handle the situation and we will. They have what they *want* now."

"They were protesting at my house, Mr Wyatt. A brick went through our window."

"Did you call the police?"

"I didn't want more trouble."

"It's unfortunate. The police would have logged the incident and it would have helped our situation. Trespass and criminal damage... bargaining chips."

"The only situation I recognize is the harassment of my family," Simon cried. "When we agreed on our plan, this wasn't even on the agenda."

Luckily for Steve Wyatt, Simon Harper could not see his raised eyes.

Was he so naïve?

The American smiled to himself... he could use that.

"Leaflets are getting dropped today explaining the benefits of fracking and the help that the villagers will receive. For god's sake, even CO_2 emissions can be reduced by up to fifty per cent! There was no need for you to arrange a public meeting, it's *your* land. You don't need *permission* from anybody to frack. We'll cancel the meeting."

"No!" Simon exclaimed. "It's alright for you, you can leave and go back to America. We have to live here when all this is all over, Mr Wyatt... and I have given them my word. The meeting will take place on December 22nd."

"Our flights are scheduled for the 21st, Mr Harper." Wyatt replied, rankled. "At this late hour, we'd have trouble changing them.; it *is* Christmas time."

"The season of goodwill, yes... except to my family. You don't need to be there," Simon declared. "I can speak to the villagers myself."

Oh no, that was not acceptable for Wyatt. Harper was already wavering and any more pressure would surely make him cave. He had to stop that from happening. The thought of being in this godforsaken country any longer than he had to filled him with dread.

Countless times he'd seen it. Interfering and threats from the resident population, or *locusts* as he called them. Once they started you had to cut them off at the source. The environmental groups would jump on the bandwagon next.

He had not lost a battle yet and was not going to lose this one. Frankly Woods would be fracked if it was the last thing he ever did.

"I will speak to Mr Carney, Mr Harper. We have almost finished our business in London. Please do not agree to anything more until I get back to you."

"I don't know..." Simon grew silent.

"If there are more problems, call me immediately; you have my cell number. Remember, as soon as it's signed, sealed and delivered, your children's future will be secure. That's what's important, nothing more. The contract is being drawn up as we speak, so please be patient."

"It's just frightening, Mr Wyatt."

"This deal will benefit us all."

"At what cost?"

"You are being *bullied,* Mr Harper and bullies should never be allowed to win. Stand up to them. *Trust me!*"

Simon pondered his words.

They *were* being bullied; his family was being intimidated. He had not thought of it that way. His blood began to boil.

Chapter Nineteen

"Take Lily with you."

Danial looked aghast. "No!"

"That is the only way that you will be leaving this house today," Ella huffed. "I don't want you on your own until this is all over, regardless of what Veronica Michaels has said."

"I'd rather eat worms," the boy cried.

"It's your sister's company or the house... your choice," Ella continued. "I have a lot to do and Lily will just get under my feet."

The thought of being accompanied outside by Lily filled Danial with horror. He could just about put up with her screeching indoors, if he could escape.

"You can build a snowman together!"

Danial's heart sank. He wanted to find Cervanae, to tell her about the protest at the hall and the hastily arranged meeting on the 22nd – but how could he with his baby sister in tow?

The situation sank in further at his mother's next few words.

"Stay close to the hall. I don't want you going anywhere near Frankly Village today."

"But Mum…"

"They are my rules!" Ella asserted.

Danial sighed deeply, knowing that he was not going to win today's argument. If Lily began to screech, he could always put his fingers in his ears. Maybe Cervanae had a magic trick to make someone silent?

The thought cheered him up no end.

So that was how he found himself playing outside with his sister.

"Be safe!" Ella smiled, dressing them both up like they were about to embark on an Arctic expedition.

Danial huffed haughtily; his mother rolled her eyes before going back inside.

Lily looked around them. "Where should we put the snowman?"

Danial did not answer. He checked his watch; it had just turned twelve. he stomped away towards the woods.

"Where are you going?" Lily cried. "Mummy said to stay close."

"Stay if you want to, I'm going to meet a friend."

"What friend?"

"She lives in the woods."

"You can't go into the woods!"

"Bye!" Danial waved farewell.

A few steps later he stopped. Lily was only six years old; anything could happen to her. The young boy sighed; he was stuck with her whether he liked it or not. He gestured frustratedly. "Are you coming?"

Lily glanced around for their mother then hesitantly followed. It was hard work trying to keep up with her brother, especially over the slippy ground. For every step of his, she had to take two, until eventually, they reached the edge of Frankly Woods. Danial began to utter a rhyme.

"Of bird, of horse, of Ox, of deer,
I call for Cervanae to appear here.
Be quick, be swift, come my way,
I need your help this very day."

It was Lily's turn to jump out of her skin at the sudden appearance of a young woman. Cervanae stood before them, her white cape cascading down to the ground. Danial moved forward and hugged his friend. "We can't stay long, but I bring you news."

"I see you bring your kin, Lily, daughter of Simon." She eyed the little girl, who now hid behind her brother.

"My Mum wouldn't let me come outside without her," Danial said sheepishly, "and I had to see you."

Cervanae smiled and held out her hand to Lily. "You are welcome, kin of Danial."

"We have to go back!" Lily said as she clung to her brother fearfully. "Mummy will be worried."

"Do not fear me, child. I mean you no harm," Cervanae smiled, trying to soothe her concern.

"She's my friend Lily. *Our* friend."

His words did not ease his sister's concern. Like Danial, stranger danger had been drummed into her, and the girl before her was certainly a stranger.

"What news?" Cervanae asked.

Danial explained all about the protest at the hall and the hastily arranged meeting taking place in Frankly Village on December 22nd.

"So, the villagers are aware?"

He nodded.

"I shall inform my friends of this progress. They will be pleased," Cervanae continued. "The villagers value nature, they respect the ancient woodland."

"More than my father, definitely."

"I shall not pit father against son," Cervanae continued. "You know his reasons; we just have to educate him – together."

She walked forward.

"Come, I will show you what is at stake."

Cervanae whispered an incantation and before their very eyes, a richly decorated sleigh appeared out of nowhere at the edge of the wood. Five reindeer stood at its helm, grunting, and barking as if eager to go.

The children's eyes nearly popped out from their heads; they had never seen such a sight.

The sleigh was adorned with lush foliage and different coloured berries, some the size of giant rubies, while others were the whitest of pearls. Soft fur coated the inside, with ivy and holly covering the exterior; sprigs of mistletoe peeked out here and there. On either side of the magnificent chariot hung two golden lanterns.

It reminded Danial of Father Christmas's sleigh. With beauty and magic like this in front of him, Danial could believe in anything – Santa Claus included.

"Climb in, children of Simon," Cervanae beckoned.

Danial scrambled in, pulling the fur up to his nose in the icy wind. Lily was more hesitant but was finally coaxed in by her brother. With a leap through the air, Cervanae placed herself astride the leading beast. "Fly, my friends!"

The reindeer stomped their hooves excitedly and soared upwards into the sky. Lily gripped onto the sleigh like her life depended on it, as if at any moment they might plummet down to the white-kissed ground far below. From their elevated position, everything appeared as miniatures beneath them, growing ever smaller the higher they flew.

An icy wind whipped at their cheeks, making their noses as red as Rudolph's as they flew ever higher. Cervanae sensed their apprehension and chuckled.

"I promise, you are both perfectly safe, children of Simon. Look around, see the beauty."

Lily tentatively obeyed, the fear that she had felt earlier now replaced by wide-eyed wonder. Both children sat mesmerized as the sleigh now flew lower, rushing over the incredible landscape that was Frankly Woods spread out beneath them.

"Do you see the animals, the birds scurrying to their homes?" Cervanae asked. The children nodded. "These ancient woodlands are home to many creatures, and must be protected."

From above, the woods looked utterly wondrous, an untouched and wild winter wonderland. The sleigh flew onwards, even swifter now over the frosty landscape. Mile after mile of white countryside stretched out like a pristine canvas beneath them. For an age, neither spoke, the overwhelming magic of the scene taking away their breath as well as their voices.

"Look children, the three hills!" Cervanae bobbed her head towards the peaks below. "A million years in the making, their steep slopes formed when this land was still covered by ice. These are the mighty Illusion Hills, with Black Tor Hill the tallest of the three. They have stood tall for many centuries."

The young boy nodded. He looked west for King Arthur's burg, where they had previously visited, pointing it out below.

"You remember, Danial, son of Simon!"

"I know how special it is!" he shouted over the rushing air, explaining all about it to Lily as they went. His sister grew braver, peering over the edge of the sleigh with her brother.

Cervanae drew their attention to yet another incredible sight. "Look below, children."

The meandering river running through the mighty peaks twisted this way and that. The reindeer suddenly dived down towards the dark water, hovering a few inches above its icy surface.

"How clear the water is – so fresh and pure," Cevanae said. "Man must not be allowed to spoil or contaminate it – not just for the sake of people, but for all the animals who dwell on its shores and in its depths. Water is their lifeblood."

Danial and Lily leaned over the side of the sleigh and dipped their fingers into the very top of the icy depths, shivering as its freezing water splashed them. The river was just beginning to ice over; though it was not solid enough to walk on yet, it would be there soon.

In one swift movement, the reindeer shot skywards again. Lily held on for dear life, before a scream of joy erupted from her mouth. Cervanae chuckled heartily astride the lead beast.

The sleigh continued, passing over farmland and the houses that dotted the frigid landscape. "Do you see how untouched this land is? Only Old Father Frost's mighty grip stirs it."

The children nodded.

"We must protect the livelihoods that are at stake." The reindeer turned swiftly on the bitter breeze. "This land cannot be polluted or fouled. Do you understand why I have shown you this?"

"If fracking takes place, there is more to be lost than just Frankly Woods!" Danial cried.

Cervanae smiled, pleased that he understood. "The wonders that you have seen, this ancient landscape... it is all far too precious to lose."

"My father mustn't do it!" The young boy looked aghast. "He will see that... he *has* to!"

"He tries to protect his family, but there are other ways to do that which will not destroy the land. Luckily, he is not so stubborn like his uncle. *You* can change his mind."

A worried look appeared on Danial's face.

"What if he won't listen?"

"We can *make* him listen."

"But how?"

"Every creature – magic or plain – will help you. All will come together to fight for our homeland and the right to live in peace."

The weight lifted from Danial's chest. He looked down, astonished to see that they were now circling high above Frankly Hall. Its standard whipped back and forth in the wind beneath them. How they had gotten back so quickly, he could not fathom... but they were home, regardless.

Before he could speak another word, the sleigh came into land on the icy parkland outside the hall. The reindeer bobbed their heads and stamped their hooves, attempting to eat the grass beneath the crushed ice – a well-deserved meal after their tiring flight.

Lily smiled, clambering out of the sleigh. She hugged Cervanae tightly. "Thank you!"

Danial followed behind her. "I think that you have a new friend."

"Always," Cervanae smiled, then her voice grew urgent. "Your mother comes, I must go."

In the blink of an eye she disappeared, the sleigh and its five reindeer following suit. Only Danial and Lily stood on the icy ground when their mother reappeared at the top of the stone steps.

The young boy braced himself for a telling-off. They'd disappeared from outside the hall and had missed lunch. He was going to be sent to his room at the very least.

But it didn't come.

"Haven't you started a snowman yet?" Ella asked. "What *have* you been up to?" She joined them on the snowy grass. "Lunch is another half an hour; come on, I'll help."

Danial looked at his watch with amazement. It was only ten minutes past twelve.

Had all that only taken *ten minutes?*

"We went—" Lily began.

"Went where?" Ella looked at her daughter.

"—to see if there was any fresh snow," Danial cut Lily off; he narrowed his eyes at her in warning.

Lily looked at her brother, then exclaimed, "We went to find snow, Mummy."

Danial sighed relieved; He was already in enough trouble with his mum. If she found out they'd been flying overhead, he'd be sent to his room until he was a hundred.

A snowball hit him. He saw his mum smirking guiltily.

Yes, he had to persuade his father to stop fracking. But for now, it could wait.

A snowball fight ensued.

Chapter Twenty

The Christmas tree sparkled.

Even Danial had to admit that it looked wonderful and festive, though he would not admit it to his mother. A warm feeling filled his belly. He loved this time of year, regardless of Lily's shrieks on Christmas morning. Dark nights snuggled up in front of a roaring fire, beautiful shining lights and baubles bestowing the house, presents... and a roast dinner topped off the season nicely.

This year though, it was different. He felt a mix of excitement and dread.

Excitement for him, dread for Cervanae.

How could he enjoy his Christmas time when she would suffer if his father won this battle? Cervanae was going to lose her home. The ancient woodland would be destroyed by fracking. A special, magical place, gone forever. He *had* to make his father see.

Danial burst headlong into the office.

Simon jumped, shocked at the unannounced intrusion. The last remnants of his coffee cup spilled over his trousers. He jumped up, wiped himself down and glared at his son.

"Danial, what have I told you about smashing into rooms like that?"

"It's *important,* Dad!"

Simon snapped back, "Unless the house is on fire or the roof has fallen in, don't shock the life out of me. I almost had a heart attack!"

"Dad, *please* don't destroy Frankly Woods!"

"Not this again," Simon said exasperatedly. "It's a piece of uninhabited woods, it's really nothing!"

"It's magic," Danial exclaimed.

Simon raised a brow, "You've been reading those fairy tales again."

"I *don't* read fairy tales," he cried, aghast, "they're for kids!"

"Aren't you a 'kid'?"

Ignoring the point, Danial continued, "Cervanae told me that the woods date back to the time of King Arthur and his knights!"

"Hasn't your mother warned you about telling lies?"

Danial did not reply straight away. How could he explain a girl who mended broken bones, could turn herself into a deer, and could even fly? He grew sheepish, deciding discretion was best when it came to magic adventures. What his parents did not know...

"She lives in the woods."

"Nobody lives in the woods!"

"There are others who live there as well; you *can't* destroy their homes!"

"So, now we have *other* imaginary friends?" His father tutted.

"There's John Barleycorn, for one!"

Simon burst out a laugh, "You made that name up!"

Danial shook his head, "I didn't, he's the wild man of the woods!"

"A *man* who *lives in the woods?*"

"There are others."

"Who?"

Danial tried to rack his brain. His father was already doubting him, so anything was better than trying to explain a talking ox and a giant horse! Before he could reply, his father spoke again.

"Are you saying that we have squatters in the woods?!"

"They are not *squatters,* it's their home – it's Cervanae's home!"

"Then they are trespassers, with no right to be there," Simon continued. "I am afraid that this unlawful resident and her cohorts – if they exist, which I very much doubt – will have to find themselves a new home. Fracking will take place and Frankly Woods will go."

"But the land, the water," Danial cried. "Fracking will destroy *all* of it."

"Who told you all this?"

"Cervanae."

"And how does this 'Cervanae' know about the fracking in the first place?"

Danial looked at the floor, sheepishly.

"Just great," Simon cried. "I told you all to keep the fracking a secret until everything was settled."

"It's her *home!*"

"You have to get your priorities right, Danial. Is it this squatter, her cohorts, or your family?" Simon puffed out frustrated. "At least I know now who's been filling your head with nonsense."

"It's *not* nonsense."

Simon ruffled the top of his head. "Do you think that I would ever put our family at risk?"

Danial shook his head.

"Or put the land that we've inherited – or the people who work on it – in jeopardy?"

"No."

"Fracking is a *good* source of energy. It is cleaner for the environment than other fossil fuel extraction methods. It will help the planet, I know it will; you just don't understand."

"But Dad," Danial pleaded, "the Spriggan said *man is poison*, and you're proving him right."

"Who?"

"The Guardian of the Fairies!"

As soon as the words left his mouth, Danial regretted them. His father looked at him strangely, with a tear in his eye. He put his fingers to his lips, silencing the boy.

"I know I'm putting a lot on young shoulders. Maybe too much for you to grasp at your age. But we don't have a money tree planted in the garden. I want to protect our future here, stay in this house and keep this land. My *only* option is fracking. It must go ahead whether we like it or not." He moved to the door. "And whether *I* like it or not, I'm going to have to change these wet trousers."

Chapter Twenty-One

"The English can't speak English," Steve Wyatt hissed.

Henry Carney's soft southern drawl responded differently, "I love their accent. It's to die for."

"Then you've spent too long in the land of the Limeys," Wyatt huffed. "You may be the owner of a multimillion-pound company, but we need to get you home, back with *normal* people".

Henry roared laughing. "I get it. You don't like the Brits?"

"I hate anyone who tries to thwart our plans... interfering cornballs!"

"Well, I always knew that you were bloodthirsty."

"That's why you hired me."

"So, do you think he'll sign?" Carney took a slug from his whiskey glass.

"He will if I have anything to do with it!" Steve Wyatt took out a contract from his briefcase.

Carney sighed deeply, "I'm not so sure. His wife has his ear. She fears for her kids and now the villagers are piling on the pressure. It's not a done deal."

"Then we just pile on more," Wyatt cried. "We bring their kids into *everything*; they're our bargaining chips. You saw the house – it needs work, a *lot* of work. His wife may have his ear, but he can't run a house on fresh air. Harper doesn't have the cash to keep it afloat long-term. One leaking roof tile would finish them off. We could even use that to our advantage and get him to accept a lower offer. Can I renegotiate?"

"No!" Henry shook his head. "I'm a man of my word. In business that means something, you still need to learn that."

"But you could save a *fortune*," Wyatt continued unabashedly. "He's desperate!"

"Stevie boy," Henry sat forward in his seat, "we will still make money on this deal."

"A *lot* of money."

Henry laughed, "Enough for you to get that expensive holiday for you and your wife."

The car turned down another windy bend and Frankly Hall came into view on top of the hill.

"I'll keep the pressure on, give him a deadline." Wyatt's excitement grew at the thought of his huge bonus. "We'll threaten to walk away unless he signs."

"We don't *want* to walk away," Henry replied. "Frankly Woods is perfect for what we want to do. We have undertaken surveys and done all the groundwork; it's the ideal spot. I don't want to have to bid again. You seem to forget that we can't move forward without the landowner's permission."

"We won't lose him, sir," Wyatt said smugly. "It's just frustrating that it would all have been done and dusted if his uncle had signed before he died."

"But he *didn't* sign, Stevie," Henry stated seriously. "We must convince Harper that the *villagers* are his enemy, not *us*. The new Lord of the Manor wants to make an impression, and that could cause us trouble. The family has to live here, and they don't want any stress, any bad feeling."

Wyatt sneered. "We'll handle those yokels, sir,"

Henry stretched out his wiry frame. They'd been in the car far too long now and he'd had enough. Being so tall didn't help him one bit, either.

"Just make sure you do. There's too much at stake for this to fail now, too much invested. And get Balkour to pile the pressure on his cohorts. He's been sitting on his heels for too long and needs to earn what we're paying him!"

Steve Wyatt pondered his boss's words as they reached the hall's iron gates. Beyond, the long, winding driveway that led up to Frankly Hall stretched far into the distance. He would make this happen, and use everything at his disposal. And God help anyone who got in his way.

***

Ella brought in the coffee tray. She couldn't trust Mrs Briggs not to throw it all over their guests if the scowl on her face was an indicator.

She poured the Texan a cup of coffee.

"Thank you, ma'am," Henry Carney smiled, bobbing his cowboy hat.

Ella poured coffee for Steve Wyatt.

"Anything but tea is a bonus," he said.

Ella laughed, "Please have some cake" then moved to check outside the office door. She scanned the long corridor beyond. Carney and Wyatt stared at her bemused; she met their gaze.

"Oh don't worry, I haven't gone mad," Ella chortled, "I'm just checking that the coast is clear."

She wouldn't be surprised to find Mrs Briggs eavesdropping outside the office door during their meeting.

"Our housekeeper is *not* a fan," Simon added.

Carney and Wyatt nodded. Now they understood the paranoia.

Ella needn't have worried about eavesdroppers at the door, however. A grating in the wall led down alongside the heating pipes towards another grill in the kitchen. Mrs Briggs sat drinking tea beside it, eagerly listening and relishing her role as detective... or, in her eyes, spy.

"I recall our first visit," Wyatt replied with a wince, "we were lucky to gain access without her barricading the door!"

A loud chuckle filled the room.

In the kitchen, Mrs Briggs's scowl came back.

"Shall we get down to business, gentlemen?" Simon asked.

Ella sat down beside him, not wanting to miss anything.

"Steve has filled me in," Carney started. "I believe that you've had some... trouble?"

"*Trouble?* that is the understatement of the year, Mr Carney!" Simon cried. "We're barred from the village, and even from the school. The children are supposed to be starting there in January and now we don't know what's happening."

"We've had protests here at the hall... and a window was smashed." Ella joined in.

"Steve said that you didn't call the police," Carney responded, looking glum. "That is unfortunate; there would be an incident number, the crime would be logged. It would have helped us greatly."

"We still have to *live* here, Mr Carney, when the fracking is done," Simon continued, "and we don't want our future life to resemble a warzone!"

"I've seen this countless times, Mr Harper," Carney said calmly as he took a swig of his coffee. "A town or village finds out about our plans and all hell breaks loose." He shook his head frustrated.

"They don't understand the technology, we have to educate them on its benefits." Carney persisted. "Fracking is a much cleaner energy source, better for the environment. Any chosen location will benefit, with funds to improve the local area."

"This is why Simon has arranged the meeting on the 22nd," Ella exclaimed. "Hopefully, you'll do a better job of explaining the benefits to the villagers, as they're just not listening to us."

"The meeting is a bad idea, Mrs Harper; it will just cause you more stress," Carney continued. "We've already dropped countless leaflets explaining the process. As the landowner, you do *not* have to inform the local residents of your plans."

"Mr Carney, we don't want to live in isolation from the local community," Ella cried. "Our children are our priority, it's all about their happiness. Anything that affects that will not be allowed to happen, even if that means cancelling this whole thing."

Carney glanced at Wyatt, who interceded.

"Fracking will secure your future here, and your children's future."

"At what cost, Mr Wyatt?" Ella cried.

The American continued, "Your children will be set up for life, they'll have no money worries and can become anything they want to be. One signature and your home and family will be secure."

He looked around them. "The hall is old. How will you pay for its upkeep if something goes wrong?"

Ella looked at Simon, concerned. It was true that something as simple as a leaking roof would finish them off and they would have to pitch a tent on the grass, unable to pay for costly repairs.

"Forget the villagers, just think of yourselves and your kids. That is all that matters," Wyatt reached into his briefcase and brought out the contract.

"We've changed our itinerary and are leaving on the red-eye flight on the 23rd. The meeting will go ahead as planned; we'll fight in your corner. It will all work out for the good."

Ella looked doubtful.

"However, there is one stipulation," Wyatt handed the contract to Simon. "We're not back in the country until February next year, so we need this signed before we head out. We need to get the ball rolling on this."

"But our solicitor—"

"Your lawyer can check it over the next few days. Time is money, and there must be a deadline. We need it signed, otherwise we'll have to walk away."

***

"You must be careful," Ella said to Simon as she shook her head. "According to Mr Carney and Mr Wyatt, your uncle was about to agree to a deal when he died." She continued tentatively, "He didn't care what the villagers thought of him, he was a recluse. But *we* live here now. You've seen how we've been treated since they found out."

"It's not been nice." Simon agreed.

"Not NICE?" Ella cried, then sighed deeply. "They welcomed us with open arms when we arrived and now, we're complete pariahs. The children are getting grief because of us alone. Where are they supposed to go to school after Christmas if not the village?

"It'll get better," Simon hugged Ella towards him. "When the villagers realize the benefits, they'll surely see that it benefits them as well."

"Will they?" Ella asked, disbelievingly. "The fracking hasn't even started yet, and look at how they're acting! Can't we just go back to how it was when we first arrived?"

Simon shook his head. "I wish that we could, but with settling uncle's debts and the inheritance tax we've had to pay, how can we afford to keep the house long-term without this offer?"

"I never thought that I would say this, but we *could* sell up, buy somewhere smaller. There would be no stress, no troubles. We'd be happy again."

"Think of the children, Ella," Simon rebuked. "This was our 'escape to the country'. A chance for the kids to run wild and play safely. Do you want to give all that up?"

Ella shook her head. "I just worry for the kids."

"We will deal with whatever comes. When we're low, almost beaten, we'll think of the kids. They'll give us the strength to carry on, fight for them alone. No one else matters."

Ella kissed her husband.

Chapter Twenty-Two

Veronica Michaels had been busy.

Leaflets had been dropped throughout the village by Shale Oil, explaining the benefits of fracking and the 'help' that the villagers would receive. Many ended up in the bin, but a few residents hesitated. There was the promise of financial help; a carrot on a stick.

Well, not a carrot exactly, more of a bribe.

Veronica had to try hard to convince the doubters. Were they going to sell out their entire village for a few miserly pounds? That would make them as bad as the oil company!

Another meeting at the pub was needed to formulate their plans, and cut the doubters off at the source. And so, the villagers found themselves back at the Green Man, the assembled crowd as noisy as ever, each with an opinion to share.

Mrs Briggs first took centre stage, relaying the news of the meeting between the Harpers and Shale Oil with gusto. Her words brought boos from the majority, whilst the doubters remained silent.

Veronica would make them see the error of their ways.

"Is the financial gain worth all the pollution and problems that fracking will cause?" She cried. "They're trying to divide us, remember that. We are stronger *together*, not apart."

"But if the village is going to be helped financially," one of Flynn Davies's cronies piped up from the back of the bar.

"Have you forgotten about the undrinkable water, the earthquakes and the traffic noise, Peter Egan? Is it worth a few miserly pounds for all that chaos?"

"Business hasn't been great recently," Egan replied. "Any financial help is a bonus, and those who say it isn't are liars."

A roar of discontent followed his words, but it was mixed with some applause.

The dividing tactic was working.

"My farm skirts Frankly Woods," Flynn Davies glared at his crony. "What damage is going to be done to my land, my animals?"

"Flynn is *right!*" Veronica cried.

It was strange for Veronica to find herself and Flynn in agreement, but it was a welcome change. She handed out thick dossiers, which stated the perils and pitfalls of fracking. Each danger was carefully listed, along with the potential damage it would do to the village.

"Verity has printed these out for me at college. We must work together, and all remain under the same consensus on the 22nd. Please read what I have discovered, and *then* let me know if you still think it is worth the bribe. Divide and conquer is practically Shale Oil's motto!"

Her words seemed to silence the doubters.

Danial won today's argument with a promise not to go into the woods or the village. He had no intention of visiting Frankly Village – meeting the Davies boys was the last thing that he wanted to do.

Lying to his parents did not come easy. It was only the fingers crossed behind his back that got him to the woods today. He sighed happily that he would see his friend as he approached the tree line.

A rustle to the left caught his attention, with an all-too- familiar loud snigger following.

Nathan Davies sneered, "Look who we have here!"

Horror filled Danial. He'd come face to face with his enemies, who emerged gleefully from behind the old stag-head oak.

He stiffened at their approach. The Davies boys surrounded him, pushing and shoving him between them like a pinball. Danial soon hit the icy ground with a thud.

"Not so quick today," Freddy laughed. "All that traitor's money weighing you down, is it?"

Danial struggled to get up, slipping and sliding on the frozen ground.

The raucous mocking laughter continued, enjoying his misfortune.

Danial tried to stand and was pushed even harder, plunging headfirst down a steep slope. Snowballs hit him from above. The laughing became louder, Nathan and Freddy enjoying their fun.

Danial was terrified. He must try to call for help.

Before he was able, a gleam of light appeared beneath the ancient oak. Behind the bullies, John Barleycorn's face and upper body followed, emerging from the old tree. Breath caught in Danial's throat.

Suddenly, a large snowball hit Nathan Davies square in the back.

The young boy spun on his heel. "Who did that?"

There was no one there; John Barleycorn had disappeared as quickly as he'd arrived.

Freddy looked up, kicking the tree hard, "It must have fallen from above."

A yell followed his words, a large snowball pelting him along with a sideswipe from a branch. Freddy spat out the snow which now covered him from head to foot.

Nathan looked wildly around them. He reached down and picked up a fallen branch to use as a weapon. "That came from no tree... come on, coward, show yourself!"

John Barleycorn's chortle floated on an icy wind.

"Only bullies are cowards!"

Freddy gripped his brother tightly. "Who said that?"

So preoccupied with the mysterious voice were they that both boys failed to notice Danial scramble unsteadily to his feet. Another giant snowball hit the two terrors, who now resembled snowmen themselves.

"You'll pay for that!" Nathan raised his weapon. "Where are you, chicken?"

The wild man of the woods materialized out of thin air before the two troublemakers, like a will-o'-the-wisp.

"I'm here!"

For a moment neither boy moved.

The Davies boys' frightened eyes took in John's leaf-covered face, with branches and vines sprouting from his various orifices. A long vine then unexpectedly twisted out from his body, like a snake being charmed out from its basket. It clasped their wrists in tight handcuffs.

"Boo!"

Nathan and Freddy howled fearfully. Both could not move, stuck firmly to the icy ground in fear.

"Do not bully Danial again," John Barleycorn smirked, "or I shall come visit you in your home!"

Fear turned to horror and the boys managed to find their feet. The shackles snapped loose and the boys' terrified screams filled the ancient woodland as they fled. Danial could not help but smile at the sight of his nemeses frantically slipping and sliding as they tried to get away as quickly as they possibly could.

"John Barleycorn!"

An angry voice made Danial's saviour turn his head. Cervanae glared at him.

"You will be in *so* much trouble when Aurochs discovers you have frightened the son of man!"

"But he helped me," Danial cried.

"Scaring young children?" Cervanae looked doubtful. "Aurochs will banish you from this woodland. I might not be able to save you this time, John."

"Nathan and Freddy Davies pushed me down, they really hurt me," Danial exclaimed. "If John Barleycorn had not come to help, things could have become even worse. Surely he can't be banished for that?"

"Bullies!" The green man hissed.

"Is this true, John?" Cervanae spoke seriously.

"Yes, I stepped in," He laughed gleefully. "I guarantee, they will not pick on anyone again."

Danial smirked. "The look on their faces when you appeared – they were so scared."

"BOO!"

Both fell about laughing.

"This is not a funny matter," Cervanae said crossly. She shook her head in dismay. "John Barleycorn, you must promise me that you will never scare those boys again; I will not inform Aurochs if you agree. Do I have your word?"

John Barleycorn nodded reluctantly.

"Now go, before I change my mind."

The wild man moved dejectedly back towards the ancient oak.

"Thank you, John, thank you for helping me," Danial spoke, stopping him in his tracks.

His leaf-covered face nodded glumly. Before slowly disappearing back into its depths, Cervanae's words brought the smile back. "Good work, John Barleycorn."

A gleeful howl filled the frigid air. With a wink of his eye, he was gone.

"John Barleycorn helped you, so will you return the favour?" Cervanae walked forward.

Danial nodded, following at her side, grateful that the green man would not get into trouble for saving him. He sighed with relief.

"Midwinter approaches; December 21st," Cervanae continued. "Every solstice, a celebration takes place, our last hurrah before the longest night. However, we are missing one vital element to make our festivity a success."

The boy looked on blankly.

"Sacred Oak Mistletoe!"

Danial was still none the wiser.

Cervanae giggled at his blank expression, "Mistletoe is magical; a sacred plant. Our ancestors have used it since time began and even today it is hallowed. Known as *All Heal*, it is believed to bestow life and growth. It grows on many trees, but oak mistletoe is the most sacred, twice as magical as that grown on other species. If found, it will add gusto to our mid-winter ceremony."

"The stag-head oak!" Danial said with wonder. He looked up. Its massive crown had died back, creating a smaller inner one, reminding him of antlers.

"An ancient tree, aeons in the making," Cervanae smiled. "Almost deer-like in appearance, isn't it? The tree has seen much of life – both good and bad – yet still stands proud. Look closely, Danial; see if there is any mistletoe for the feast."

"What does mistletoe look like?"

"Look for pointy leaves, forked branches with white or red berries. Mistletoe rarely grows in woodlands, so we must search hard."

Danial moved quickly around the stag-head oak but couldn't see anything out of the ordinary. He shook his head disappointed.

"The oak tree is the king of trees. But the woods are made up from many trees, as you can see," Cervanae gestured around them. "Each has its significance and importance."

"But, how can you tell them apart?" Danial asked.

"I will teach you," Cervanae moved quickly to the edge of the ancient woodland. She stopped beside a magnificent specimen; its long crooked branches spread out high above.

"Ah, a young oak. Can you see the difference?"

Danial looked up at the mighty beast, its acorn cups and carpet of frozen leaves clinging on for dear life. There were more branches all over, startlingly different to the stag-head oak with its heavy crown of wood.

Cervanae walked around its trunk, checking as she went. "Many would say that Mistletoe is a parasite, but others know it to be magical." She sighed disappointedly, "No, nothing here."

Onwards they moved to the next tree, Cervanae giving lessons as they went.

"Behold, the sacred ash tree, and yonder is the willow."

"The ash is the tree of strength and is known as the *world tree*. It links the past, present and future; the underworld, middle earth and the realm of spirits."

Danial stared up at the ash's branches just visible beneath a thin layer of hard ice. Cervanae moved on, checking as she did. There was no mistletoe there.

"Here we have the willow, a tree of enchantment and wishes, its groves always magical."

Danial's eyes grew as wide as saucers. *A tree of wishes...*

Cervanae chuckled again. "You may ask the willow to grant your wish by tying a knot around a branch. If granted, you must return to the tree, untie the knot and thank the tree by leaving a gift in gratitude."

"*Any* wish?" Danial asked amazed.

"Any." Cervanae checked the tree but again was left disappointed.

Deeper into the icy gloom they travelled, the young boy a keen follower.

"Look, here is the birch tree or the *lady of the forest*," Cervanae smiled, "she influences Christmas time and beyond. A truly special tree."

Danial took in the birch's pale bark that shone like silver in the low light. Again, Cervanae scanned the tree for mistletoe without success.

Onwards they moved. Danial learned about the yew, sycamore, hazel, and many more besides until they had circled back to where they had started, beside the stag-head oak.

Each story was as fascinating as the last. The history and myth of each tree made Danial even more determined to save the woods from the destruction that fracking would bring.

Cervanae began to circle the mighty oak once again.

"Have you checked *every* nook and cranny... even beneath the ice? Sometimes it likes to hide away."

Danial nodded, eyes scanning for any sign of the scarce cutting. He checked again, inspecting every inch, running his fingers over the rough bark, feeling in small hollows that had formed over the years.

"Luck does not favour us today," Cervanae sighed disappointedly, about to give up.

The young boy cried out excitedly. "Here!" He pulled a small sprig from a low-lying branch that had been laying on the ground, covered with ice. "Is this it?"

Cervanae clapped her hands in delight. "Well done, Danial, son of Simon."

He beamed at his success, mightily pleased to have been able to help Cervanae in her search.

He carefully handed the precious cargo to his friend, who took it gladly.

"All is now set for—"

"The midwinter feast!" Danial exclaimed, not yet understanding what the feast entailed.

"And you shall be our guest of honour," Cervanae glowed happily. "Two days hence, come back here to the woods. Repeat the verse that I have taught you and I will come for you."

Danial looked worried, "My parents will never allow—"

"Out of the mouths of babes," Cervanae said, reading his thoughts before he could even speak them. "So we must find another way."

"How?" Danial asked nervously, not understanding what she meant.

Cervanae smiled knowingly but said no more.

Chapter Twenty-Three

"Do you think Danial needs to talk to someone?" Simon asked Ella, concerned.

"Why?"

"These imaginary friends are becoming a regular occurrence. He was talking about one called John Barleycorn and another – the Spriggan – the other day."

"Who?"

"The 'wild man of the woods' and the 'guardian of the fairies' apparently," Simon replied.

Ella's chuckled.

"That was exactly my response. He's too old for imaginary friends and is just talking nonsense."

Ella's gaze fell on their daughter, who was having a tea party with her toys beside the Christmas tree.

"Lily has them now, but she'll grow out of the habit soon. Why has Danial not done so?"

Lily was in deep conversation with a teddy bear.

"Danial misses his mates back home. He'll make new friends; it'll pass."

"I hope it does... and soon," Simon huffed. "He slammed into my office today, scaring the wits out of me. *'I have to save the woods, save Cervanae's home'*"

Lily looked up from her toys, "But she'll have nowhere to live, Daddy."

Simon and Ella looked at each other, surprised. Ella walked over to their daughter, who was now pouring out a cup of tea for teddy.

"What do you know about Danial's friend, Lily?"

"She lives in the woods."

Ella's eyes grew narrow and her heart began to pound hard.

"Where in the woods?" Simon followed his wife.

Lily remembered Danial's shake of the head and hesitated. "Uhhh... *nowhere?*"

She grew silent.

Simon sat down beside the little girl.

"Lily?"

Nothing.

"You're not in any trouble, but if there *is* a woman in the woods, we need to know about her. Keeping secrets is wrong."

Lily was at heart a good girl, and the words soon tumbled from her mouth. "She was really nice. We went on a sleigh ride."

"A *sleigh ride?*" Ella looked alarmed. "And when did you go to the woods?"

Lily grew timid, fearful that she'd get into trouble. She muttered her words. "I went to meet her with Danial when we built a snowman."

Fear gripped Ella. *Danial was speaking the truth!*

"How many times have we warned you about stranger danger, Lily?" Simon said sharply.

"She didn't hurt us, Daddy." His daughter looked at him. "We flew all over the woods. It was fun!"

Both parents stared at each other. Now it was Lily's turn to talk nonsense.

"You're *not* to go back to the woods again, do you understand me?" Ella chided. "Danial too."

Lily nodded sheepishly.

***

More trouble greeted Danial as he returned home. 'Out of the mouths of babes, out of the mouth of Lily'. He finally understood Cervanae's words.

His parents' anger exploded.

Regardless of whether they'd believed fantastic stories of healed bones and flying sleighs, disobeying them did *not* go down well, and he was the main culprit.

He was told off royally for taking Lily to meet a stranger in the woods.

Banned from visiting there again.

Banned from going out by himself.

Sent to his room.

The thought of never being able to see Cervanae again filled him with dread. It was better when they'd *not* believed him, and simply thought he was lying.

At least then there were ways he could see his only friend.

Danial dropped down heavily onto his bed, misery engulfing him in a huge wave. Seeing Cervanae was the only joy he'd had since they had moved here, to the back of beyond. He had learned so many things from her; he had been taught about the wonders of nature.

And what about the midwinter feast? Danial was the guest of honour. If he was barred from leaving the house... what would happen then?

Why did he have to take Lily with him?

That thought filled his brain until he was called down for lunch.

It was not a pleasant meal; his parents were still angry with him, and Lily was unusually quiet. That was how the next two days panned out – his mum and dad's wrath abating slowly, and Lily quietly apologetic for dropping him in it.

The only saving grace was that it was Christmas. The abundance of festive decorations cheered him up no end, the tree wonderful with its lights shining – a magical sight to see.

Yet it was tinged with sadness at the thought that Cervanae and her friends were going to lose their home, but Danial knew for sure that now was not the right time to bring it up with his parents.

He was called downstairs to help many times in preparation for Christmas Day, told that his dad was busy on a secret task.

He helped to wrap presents.

He helped replace decorations that had seen better days.

He brushed up the thousands of needles that had fallen from the tree... a never-ending job that he neither relished nor enjoyed.

There *were* positives, though.

The highlight was making Christmas cookies with his mum and sister. He had fun and – for once – enjoyed their company.

Ella smiled, grateful to have her children safely around her. "We'll make some for the tree!"

Danial made a deer-shaped cookie in honour of his friend. Luckily for him, Lily had not seen Cervanae's deer form, and he was not going to share this information with anybody; he'd be banned from going out for a thousand years!

All this work did take his mind somewhat off Cervanae. It would have been impossible to escape his mum's watchful gaze, anyway.

The easterly wind was dropping the temperature like a stone.

Later, Danial's father returned from his hush-hush mission, looking like a frozen icicle.

He shook his head. "Nobody!"

Ella sighed, relieved. "You walked the whole of the woods?"

Danial's ears pricked at the mention of Cervanae's home.

"No... too cold!" Simon shook his head, warming himself beside the fire. "I managed half of it; I'll finish the rest tomorrow. Hopefully, by then the weather may have eased up a bit."

Ella looked disappointed, but her husband's blue-tinged complexion brought some closure... for today, at least.

"So far, it's completely clear," Simon continued. "No one lives there, no squatters at all."

Both parents felt a surge of relief. They'd have to put it down to children's imaginations, not some odd stranger after all. Anyway, they would find out for sure tomorrow... weather permitting, that was.

If it was anything like today though, they'd all be staying indoors, Simon's reconnoitring expedition cancelled for another day.

The snow was still falling heavily.

It was the coldest December on record, so the news channel reported. Danial could well believe it... even *inside* the hall it was icy, and any chance of escaping was zero.

If his dad was anything to go by however, today he was glad to be inside.

He just hoped Cervanae had a plan.

Chapter Twenty-Four

The next day was the same as the last.

To keep them busy, Ella decided to go from room to room, sorting things into three piles: keep, bin and charity. It wasn't a particularly festive activity, but in the end it was more interesting than Danial had thought it was going to be.

They started on the very bottom floor and worked their way up. Each room was different from the last. Danial did not remember half of it, since he'd last explored the house when they first moved in. Apart from the rooms that they used regularly, he discovered a cellar, a drawing room, a games room, a music room and many more beyond.

Every room took around half an hour to sort through; some took longer, especially when the trio reached the second floor.

What could only be described as a junk room greeted them. Danial looked on in dismay... this would take all day!

Regardless, Ella plugged on, sorting piles into their different categories. Two hours later they had in fact reached the fireplace. But even though things were sorted, the room still looked like a tornado had just blown through it.

The mantelpiece was truly stunning for a simple bedroom; it was engraved stone, with intricate carvings of hunting scenes adorning it. Danial moved forwards examining it. "What's this?"

He pulled a small iron ring hidden under the lip of the mantelpiece. Immediately a creaking sound started, growing louder with each passing second.

"What did you *do?*" Ella cried, fearful that the ceiling was about to cave in. She pulled the children close to her for protection. To their astonishment, a large panel at the side of the stone fireplace scraped open, revealing a secret passageway beyond.

For a moment, nobody moved; their eyes stared into the dark entrance, surrounded with its years of dust and cobwebs. Beyond, the top of some stone steps could be seen.

"Danial, could you ask Mrs Briggs to come up here?" his mother cried, not daring to move.

The boy shook his head, "No way... I'm not missing this, there could be pirate treasure hidden down there!"

Ella raised her eyes, too preoccupied to answer. She repeated the same request to Lily, who flew out of the room like the wind. For what felt like an age they waited, Ella holding an impatient Danial back. A creaking on the stairs told them that Mrs Briggs was nearby. Within a few moments, the old woman appeared at the door.

"You called for me?" She spoke breathlessly, the steep stairs not helping her wheezing.

Ella pointed ahead. "Do you know about *that?*"

Mrs Briggs followed the direction of her pointed finger to the secret doorway.

"Well I never," She uttered with astonishment, her eyes taking in the sight. "I've worked here almost sixty years and this is the first time I have ever seen that doorway."

"Did Mr Harper-Fox ever mention it?" Ella enquired, still holding onto Danial, who was chomping at the bit to explore.

Mrs Briggs shook her head. "I don't believe he knew anything about it. This was his junk room, nothing more."

"Well, there certainly appears to be more than junk in here!" Ella replied, still not quite believing what she was seeing.

"Are you going to take a look, then?" the old woman asked as she peered down into the darkness.

"Yes!" Danial shouted as he tried to break free, but his mother was still holding him firm.

"We should wait for your father before exploring."

Danial looked disappointed. How long his dad might be, he didn't know – but he wanted to explore... and explore *now*.

Thankfully for Danial, he didn't have long to wait. Simon soon appeared at the bedroom door, rubbing his hands together for warmth, his cheeks and nose a bright rosy red.

"Lily told me I had to come upstairs as quickly as possible. What's going on?"

"We've found something amazing!" Danial said excitedly as he finally freed himself from his mother, waving at the secret passageway that had opened up.

Simon's mouth dropped open and his eyes opened wide. "What the—"

A quick cough from Ella stopped him from completing the sentence.

"I mean... what in *heaven's name* is that?"

"It's a secret passage," Danial cried excitedly.

"We don't know *what* it is, exactly," Ella countered, logic and sense taking over. "We found it when we sorted the room."

Simon looked around them at the pile of bin bags filled to the top with what could only be described as *stuff*. "You say you've been *sorting* it? It doesn't—"

Ella glared at him. Simon backtracked once again.

"It... uhh... looks like you've done a great job." He kissed the top of her head and smiled. No one else could see the fingers tightly crossed behind his back.

Danial was becoming even more impatient. "Can we explore now?"

"It looks ever so dark in there," Mrs Briggs noted. "There are a couple of flashlights in the kitchen for when the generator fails.

Simon ran down to the kitchen, then flew back up the stairs as fast as his legs would carry him. He now stood back in the room, breathless but with the two torches in hand.

Lily, who had followed closely behind her father, peeked around him, not *really* wanting to find out what was in the scary, dark tunnel – after all, there *could* be ghosts!

"Would you watch the children, please?" Ella asked Mrs Briggs, who nodded as Simon approached the passageway, shining a torch down the steep stone steps.

"I'm coming too," Danial affirmed, following behind his dad.

Ella tried to stop him. "It might not be safe."

"He can go between us," Simon accepted, handing the second torch to his wife. He then picked up a candlestick from the mantelpiece, in case he needed to use it as a weapon. "Remember the motto of the Scouts: *be prepared*," he said, somewhat grimly.

Simon then stepped tentatively through the secret entrance, the sturdy candlestick gripped firmly in his hand. Danial was but a step behind, desperately trying to see around his father. He wondered if there might be some secret treasure hidden in the passageway.

Sadly, there wasn't.

As they progressed along the dark corridor it seemed to descend lower and lower, the light from their torches struggling against the darkness.

The group reached what seemed to be a small doorway carved into the rock. Simon held the candlestick above his head and carefully pushed it open.

Their torches lit up a tiny space beyond. It couldn't really be called a *room* as you could barely swing a cat in it. Ella peered over Simon's shoulder to get a better view.

"What's in it?"

"Treasure?" Danial asked excitedly... but was left disappointed by his father's reply.

"Well... it looks like there's a small seat carved into the rock, a candle, a book and a small glass container."

This unusual collection of objects momentarily silenced Danial and Ella. Simon approached the seat, stooping down because of the low ceiling.

He reached for the book, its pages brown and tatty with age. It quickly became clear what kind of book it was. "It's a bible," Simon exclaimed.

"This must be a priest hole then," Ella gasped.

"A *priest hole?*" Danial repeated, looking at his mother inquisitively. It was a phrase that he had never heard before.

"Hundreds of years ago, Catholics were persecuted because of their religion; authorities hunted them down and put them in jail. If their owners were Catholic, some large houses – like Frankly Hall – would hold secret services for their inhabitants and other trusted adherents to the faith. If those in power caught wind of such a gathering, the King's men would be sent to capture the priest who would officiate the religious ceremony. Because of this, the owners built hidden passages and even rooms where a priest could hide in such emergency situations. After all, if a Catholic priest was caught, he would almost certainly be put to death.

Although stories of secret passages and King's men fascinated Danial, it wasn't quite the 'secret treasure' that he'd had in mind.

"It looks ancient," Simon exclaimed as he examined the book. It had certainly seen far better days and had no doubt fed a few mice over the years if the tattered page edges were anything to go by.

He then took a closer look at the glass container. "It's got burnt wood inside," he mused, "that's a little strange."

"Maybe it's a holy relic," suggested Ella. "The priests did have such things, so please *be careful with it*. We don't want to offend any higher power!"

Simon chuckled, but nervously obeyed, carefully replacing the fragile container back to its position on top of the seat. After all, fighting with the villagers was bad enough; he didn't want to have to face the wrath of anyone else.

"Look – the steps continue down," Ella said as she shone her torch into the darkness below. She gestured to Simon, "You first..."

"I thought it was always supposed to be *women and children* first?"

"Not when we're exploring the unknown, *darling.*"

Simon sighed, putting down the bible. He carefully trod down the steps, descending deeper and deeper into the gloom until finally the tunnel levelled out.

He swept the torch left and right, up and down. Suddenly the light illuminated a huge rat – as big as a housecat, no less – which was momentarily startled before scurrying back into the darkness.

Ella screamed, turning around to face the way they came. "Stay with your father," she ordered Danial, before sprinting up the stairs as fast as she could.

Simon and Danial stood stock still for a moment, both trying to figure out whether the rat might attack from the darkness into which it had retreated. In the silence they could hear a faint roar coming from further along the tunnel.

"It's getting to dangerous; we should head back now," Simon suggested, his voice becoming firm.

"But Dad, *look,*" Danial pointed ahead. "Can you see that?"

Lowering his torch, Simon could make out a pinprick of light glowing at what must be the tunnel's end.

Simon was now torn. His fearful side wanted to run away – and run *now*. Yet the brave part of him – the one that he preferred Danial to see – was just as determined to solve the mystery of the passage as was his son.

Bravery won out.

"Cover your neck," Simon warned.

Danial looked confused.

"Rat's jump – they'll go for your throat."

Danial wasn't entirely sure that this was true, but still followed his father forward with caution. "Come on Dad, hurry up," he urged.

"No! Slow down; tread carefully," his father snapped, the bravery running out as rapidly as it had appeared. Every step felt like being welcomed into the abyss by an evil lurking within.

At the next step Simon took, a loud scratching and scurrying startled him. He fell backwards, dropping the candlestick; the torch was thrown up into the air thus equalling his momentum. Scrambling back to his feet, kung fu stance at the ready, he reached up for the spinning, arcing torch but only succeeded in grabbing at the beam of light. The torch bounced off his arm and fell to the floor, extinguishing its brightness.

Danial stepped past his father, deciding to run as quickly as he could towards the light. With every step his heart beat faster, expectations increasing that a rat would attack him at any moment. The temperature was also plummeting the closer he got to the end of the passage. Eventually he reached a pile of rocks which led up towards a large circle of light. He began to climb.

An icy wind whistled past him back into the tunnel. Danial clambered up, up, up into the light and gasped.

In front of him was a flowing river. Three hills rose above, one towering mightily high.

Black Tor Hill!

Looking further around him, Danial could see Frankly Hall in the distance.

Disappointment welled up inside him.

There was no treasure.

There were no pirates.

He felt a faint glimmer of hope as he wondered whether the tunnel was built for smugglers, but as his father now caught up with him, the hope rapidly faded.

"Just great – *more* expense," said Simon.

Danial looked at him blankly.

"If *we* can get *out*, then *others* could get *in!*"

Danial started to see the problem.

Simon continued, "We're going to have to install a barricade or gate to stop any potential intruders." He sighed wearily, "I don't want to be in bed at night with robbers searching the house! Looks like we'll have to prune even more money from the money tree…"

Chapter Twenty-Five

Danial yawned loudly.

December 21st had dragged on, despite it technically being the shortest day of the year. The minutes ticked by, now seemingly even slower after the disappointment of the secret tunnel.

Danial had overheard a conversation between his parents; his father had searched the rest of the woods and had found no trace of Cervanae nor anyone else for that matter. Now he worried that his friend might have left him alone; the thought filled him with dread.

Throughout the evening he had stared up at his ceiling, hoping that it would disappear like it had before, with Cervanae materialising in a bedroom snowscape. Much to his continued disappointment however, it remained fixedly in place.

Simon and Ella had checked in on him a few times, but had since gone to bed themselves. Frankly Hall was now quiet, except for the creaking of the floorboards as the house settled. Danial's eyes closed; although he desperately wanted to see his friend, the tiredness finally overcame him. He drifted into a comfortable sleep, colourful dreams slowly washing away the dark—

"Hng!" Danial snorted as he woke up with a start. What time was it? He couldn't tell. Groggily opening his eyes, he noticed that his bedroom door was slightly ajar; perhaps the cold draught blowing through was what had awoken him.

He pulled the covers tightly around him, shuffling towards the bedroom door to close it, looking all the while like a linen-encased mummy.

Danial scanned the darkened hallway beyond for any sign of Cervanae, but there was none. He could, however, see a slim crack of light gleaming from his parent's bedroom door. He would have to be careful if his friend did turn up.

Huffing his frustration, Danial returned reluctantly to his bed, but as he was about to climb back on it, he gasped in shock. On top of his pillow sat a small bottle, its contents shining magically in the gloom.

He read the attached label:

Drink me all down in one,
A mirror will aid the midwinter fun.

A *mirror?* Danial pondered the writing confused. He thought for a moment and then moved quickly to the long mirror attached to the wardrobe door and stared intently into it, and...

...nothing happened.

"Cervanae?" he called gently.

Again, nothing.

He thought for a moment, then read the bottle again. It had to be from his friend, he *knew* it. But what to do?

Gingerly, Danial took a sip from the shining bottle. He had expected it to taste sweet, like the bubblegum concoction that had warmed him in the forest. But this liquid was tart, reminding Danial of strong mint sauce. He took a deep breath before downing the remainder in one.

He sat back on his bed, for a moment feeling nothing strange at all.

But then it began.

His left arm jerked slightly, followed by his left leg. His right arm and leg were next, then the rest of his body followed as if something was being tugged from deep inside him. Danial let out a sneeze, then a gasp as he saw what was sitting beside him on the bed.

It was his double!

Danial blinked.

The double blinked back.

"You're me!" Danial stammered, completely shocked to find an identical twin seated on his bed.

"No, you're *me!*" the double answered.

Both boys stood up as if in unison. They followed each other around the room in a seemingly never-ending circle, each looking the other up and down. Danial took in the other boy's pyjamas, his unkempt bed hair and his favourite team's football slippers on the boy's feet. He was stunned, truly astonished. A duplicate boy stood in his bedroom, as perfect as if Danial was looking in a mirror... only the mirror could answer back!

Now he understood the label on the potion.

Danial bent over. The double followed. He raised his arm and the opposite arm shot up from the other boy. Amused, he continued in the same vein for five minutes, trying out his double's response to Danial moving his fingers, legs, and even tongue.

Though Danial found the situation funny, it seemed that his double did not. The fifth time Danial waved his leg around and laughed at how silly his mirror-self looked, his double let out a *tut* of approval which made Danial freeze in place, leg still in the air.

"Have you finished?" the double sighed.

Danial nodded sheepishly and the two boys lowered their respective legs.

"Thank you," said the double, the tone of his voice a little condescending. He stared at Danial wearily, as if a bothersome pest was annoying him. "You must be swift; you have things to do."

"What things?"

The double raised its eyes, genuinely surprised.

"Mother Christmas awaits your presence, do you not remember?"

"Cervanae!"

The amusement of having a double had somehow caused Danial to forgot he had somewhere to be. He ran over to his wardrobe and pulled out some clothes. This time the double did not mirror his actions; he just stood still and repeated a verse over and over:

"The midwinter feast is here, be on your way,
It's time to celebrate the shortest day.
When the clock strikes one, I will be done,
Your bed shall be empty and I shall be gone."

Danial did not need telling twice. He quickly dressed, his double still repeating his rhyme. The double then climbed into bed and pulled the covers up around him. A wave of relief washed over Danial; if his parents were to check in on him now, everything would look perfectly normal – meaning he could get out of the house!

In the blink of an eye, Danial quietly sneaked out onto the landing. The sliver of light from his parent's bedroom lit up the darkened passageway just enough for him to avoid any obstacles.

It was nigh on impossible to avoid making any noise when descending the large staircase; the old wood creaked loudly with every step. Another way of getting downstairs was needed if Danial was to avoid waking anyone up – he certainly couldn't risk anyone seeing both him *and* his double!

Danial suddenly had an idea. He climbed onto the banister and slid silently down it to the floor below. He stood quietly at the bottom of the stairs for a minute or two, listening for any signs of movement from upstairs.

There was none.

He tip-toed over to the doorway that led down into the kitchen, gently descending the steps one-by-one. He then crept towards the back door, knowing that exiting through the front would wake up the entire household.

As he opened the heavy door, cold frosty air hit him instantly. The Beast from the East still held the country in its icy grip.

Danial stepped through the threshold and gently pulled the door shut behind him, his breath clearly visible in the freezing cold air.

The heavens above shone with a mass of beautiful stars twinkling brightly in the dark night sky. Orion – the mighty warrior – stood proudly overhead, as it had done for many a millennia.

A misty halo could be seen highlighting the moon, giving the bright orb the appearance of a saint in a painting from long ago.

Danial stole across the ground, a fresh coating of snow not helping his journey. Stiff due to the frigid air, he slipped and slid more than once during his dash to Frankly Woods.

Chapter Twenty-Six

Finally Danial reached his destination and without a moment's rest began to recite the verse he had been taught, concentrating hard to ensure he used the correct words

> "Of bird, of horse, of Ox, of deer,
> I call for Cervanae to appear here.
> Be quick, be swift, come my way,
> I need your help this very day."

In the blink of an eye, Cervanae appeared beside him, her flickering torch giving colour and warmth to the area around them. Danial hugged his friend tightly and a smile spread across both their faces, joyful to see each other.

"Come, the night wanes fast!"

He followed eagerly behind the flickering light, its flame illuminating the snowy landscape. Ahead he heard voices. Danial quickened his pace, anxious to see what lay beyond the large stag-head oak.

His eyes grew wide at the spectacle that greeted them. Beyond the clearing, a huge bonfire burned brightly, tall flames reaching up as if trying to touch the stars. Holly, Ivy and Mistletoe draped snowy branches.

Lanterns hung from trees. Gifts sparkled brightly beneath bare branches.

All those that he'd met previously were gathered around; Aurochs walking around haughtily, Tarpan looking on at the festivities with the other excitable animals – and he was especially pleased to see John Barleycorn, who bobbed his leaf-covered head in recognition. Danial waved back, grateful to see his saviour. Mab, Oberon, and the entire hoard of greenies swooped around him in rapturous greeting.

"You are very welcome this special night, young master," Oberon smiled, his delicate cape floating around him. "Tonight we celebrate midwinter, the feast day of our beloved Mother Christmas."

Danial bowed to the King and Queen of the Fairies and with the respect he knew it deserved replied, "Thank you."

Cervanae approached Aurochs, though for a moment Danial did not follow. He checked all around, expecting at any moment for the Spriggan to jump out at him; her last welcome had not exactly been friendly.

Nothing.

Sighing with relief, Danial caught up with his friend. Aurochs looked him up and down but did not pass comment on his presence; instead the huge ox bowed its head and addressed Cervanae.

"Greetings Mother Christmas. We await a few more latecomers, then the burning of the Yule log shall commence."

Cervanae smiled. "Danial, I would like you to meet a few creatures that you have not seen yet; they come especially from slumber."

Danial followed her gaze towards the ground. Below, a hedgehog and dormouse looked up at him curiously, their families gathered around them in a tight mass to keep warm. He was amazed to see each creature wrapped in a tiny blanket as if they had just gotten up from their beds. Cervanae nodded to both.

"Albi, Hazel; greetings. I am truly honoured that you and your kin interrupt your rest to celebrate with me."

The hedgehog yawned loudly then spoke.

"Midwinter comes but once a year; we cannot miss it no matter how tired we feel."

"He 'cannot miss' the feast that will follow!" Hazel the dormouse puffed, her long tail and thin black whiskers twitching with amusement.

Danial stood in awe. The sight of talking animals was still a wonder to behold, even though he should be quite used to it by now.

"You bring a guest I see, Mother Christmas," Albi continued, ignored the tiny mouse beside him.

"This is Danial, son of Simon," Cervanae replied as she gestured to the boy.

"Son of *man*," the hedgehog countered.

Danial took another look at the small creature; what astounded him was that the hedgehog had no spikes.

"When they go to bed they remove their coats," Cervanae clarified, reading his thoughts.

Albi nodded in confirmation, yawning once more.

"It would be very uncomfortable if we kept them on; they're hung up until spring so we can snuggle in our beds. A blanket will suffice tonight though, as it is such a fuss and bother to put our suit of armour back on... especially when one has just woken up."

A group of hedgehogs standing behind Albi all nodded their agreement, huddling closer against the cold.

Hazel snorted; she'd never had to take off a heavy coat of spikes and had neither the understanding nor patience to put up with the moaning hedgehogs. She looked all around then asked, "Are we ready to start?"

"Just the Otterleys to come," Cervanae said.

Danial could hear a chirping-like noise, increasing in volume as whatever was making it approached.

"Ah, they arrive," his friend smiled.

Danial let out a gasp as a family of wild otters emerged from the snowy undergrowth. There were fathers, mothers, babies, aunts... simply too many individuals to count. He laughed as the babies skidded over the ice on their bellies, enjoying the winter wonderland as he might with his own family.

For a brief moment, a sense guilt overcame Danial as he thought of happy times playing in the snow with his mum and dad – sledging, throwing snowballs, building snowmen and even playing with Lily. He'd been hard on his parents lately, especially his father. But how could he make him see sense if he would not listen?

The sound of Cervanae's voice brought him back to the present.

"Good evening, Mr Otterley."

The head otter stopped in front of them and bowed his head. His fur was brown, with a distinctive pale circle on top of the crown.

The chirps continued, even louder now.

"Apologies for our tardiness, Mother Christmas," the father said, raising his voice over the din, "the pups needed feeding… and as you can see by their size, they are greedy little tykes. We hope that we haven't delayed proceedings *too* much."

The otter's eyes then fell onto Danial and narrowed sharply; Cervanae recognised the look.

"Do not fear for yourself or your family. Danial may well be a son of man, but he is a kind boy and is willing to help."

Mr Otterley raised his eyebrows doubtfully; his wife moved forward tentatively, whispered a reprimand in his ear and then spoke with a kind voice.

"Welcome, Danial, son of man. Please forgive my husband's wariness; your species has not exactly been our friend. However, if Mother Christmas is happy to vouch for you then that is good enough for me."

She shook Danial's hand, then turned her head towards the other otters. "Come children," she said, "come and meet the son of man."

The pups needed no further encouragement and skidded towards him happily, chirping all the way. Danial was sure he could hear words he recognised amongst the more animal sounds, but nothing that made any real sense.

Mrs Otterley giggled, explaining, "They have not quite grasped human language yet, chirping more than they talk."

"Just as it should be, I would say," Danial replied.

A huge smile spread across both the mother and father's face at his words.

The pups rolled and played in the snow, gesturing for Danial to join them. Though tempting, Danial knew that should his parents find his clothes dirty and wet he'd be in serious trouble; he gently refused the offer so as not to upset.

"Come now; we must begin the Solstice," the ever-serious Aurochs boomed. "If we do not hurry, midnight will be upon us and the midwinter festival will be gone once more."

Mrs Otterley whispered to her babies, who immediately quietened.

Looking mightily pleased with himself, the ox strode slowly and pompously towards a large log set on the ground beside the bonfire. He raised his head proudly and began to speak.

"Welcome, nature spirits, my dear friends. This midwinter day, we rejoice at the return of the sun from the cold and dark. It is the longest night, on which celebrate Yuletide, the turning point between the old and new year. We also rejoice in the feast day of Mother Christmas."

At these words, the assembled animals bowed as one towards Cervanae.

"Through the performance of these solemn rituals, we follow in the footsteps of our ancestors," Aurochs continued, "so let the burning of the sacred Yule log begin."

Cervanae joined Aurochs beside the fire, which was flickering to and fro in the icy breeze. Danial saw Oberon fly towards them, carrying what looked like a piece of burning cinder. He carefully handed it to Cervanae, bowing deeply before flying back to rejoin Mab and the rest of the greenies.

Cervanae bent down gracefully, placing the smoking token atop the large log that lay on the ground. She whispered an incantation that Danial could not quite make out and within a matter of seconds, the log began to smoke, with wispy ghost-like tentacles swirling up from its base.

"Spirits of the forest," Cervanae announced loudly and clearly, "ancient elementals born of nature; I light this Yule log with our most precious remains from last year."

She picked up a goblet set beside the log and raised it high in the air.

"I toast to good harvests, to good health, to those no longer with us, to our triumph over winter and to the rebirth of spring. May this sacred offering bring good luck and the protection of our ancient woodland and all its creatures within."

Cervanae sipped from the goblet. As she did so, a cacophony of noise erupted. The birds squawked, the otters chirped, there was chittering and chattering, clacking and clattering, everyone confirming the toast in the loudest way possible. John Barleycorn hurrahed loudly as he jumped around with wild and boundless energy.

"To the forest!" Danial shouted joyfully, the huge wave of happiness and celebration engulfing him completely. Cervanae beckoned him to join her by the fire, handing him another goblet as he did so.

"Drink, celebrate with us!"

Danial took a sip of the clear liquid and a huge smile spread across his face. A heady mix of marshmallow, butterscotch, cinnamon, toffee and other sweet flavours combined together into the most amazing taste which filled his mouth; quickly, he took a larger gulp.

"The sacred Yule log shall burn until dawn arrives," Cervanae announced as she raised her goblet once again, "so let the feast begin!"

The merrymakers didn't need telling twice.

A throng of creatures approached an enormous pile of presents, each taking a single gift labelled with their name. Excitement and chatter filled the air as the boxes and bags were opened with delight.

"This is for you," Cervanae said as she handed Danial a small parcel wrapped in silk.

"But I have nothing for you," he replied, feeling guilt and frustration. Why had he not brought something for her? It was Cervanae's feast day, and yet the thought had not even crossed his mind.

"I do not require material gifts, Danial, son of Simon. Your presence here is bestowal enough!"

Danial unwrapped his present, still feeling rather remorseful. It was a clear glass bauble that twinkled brightly as he held it up to take a closer look. The trinket was half-filled with water, on the surface of which a beautiful shining light was floating."

"You have a moon glade," Cervanae smiled.

Danial looked at his friend quizzically as he repeated her words, "A *moon glade?*"

"A flash of moonlight reflecting on the water is called a moon glade, or as some may call it a moon wake. Wherever you may be, so will this fragment of a moonbeam. It will always point north, lighting your way as you walk. Whenever there is a moonlit sky, the glow from the glade is there to help you."

A huge smile spread across Danial's face. He hugged Cervanae, saying "Thank you" with all his heart.

Danial then held the bauble in front of him as he turned this way and that. He saw how the sliver of light always shifted northwards like a compass no matter which way he himself faced. How did one capture a moonbeam? And how did it know where to point to? It was magic upon magic.

Cervanae laughed gleefully at the wonder she could see on Danial's face. "Now, let us eat," she said.

With a swish of her hand, a sumptuous feast appeared on laden tables, each one set at the perfect height for the guest whose place it was.

Hazel the dormouse had been right about Albi; the hedgehog was first to take a seat, gulping down mouthful after mouthful of the incredible banquet.

Cervanae took Danial's hand and led him to his seat, of course next to hers. In front of them there were sausage rolls, cake, jelly, apple pie with custard, and even a large chocolate Santa; his glass was already filled with cream soda. The smile on Danial's face was so wide – he couldn't believe how all his favourite things to eat and drink were laid out before him like this.

Rather like Albi, Danial couldn't stop himself from wolfing down so much so quickly that he soon felt more than a little queasy. He hadn't yet tried the apple pie, but would have to leave it until later.

To one side of the clearing, joyous music started up; the greenies were playing flute and harps and even some instruments Danial didn't even recognise. A roar of approval greeted the song, with many getting up to dance and sing along.

Everyone knows that time passes extremely quickly when you're having fun, and so it was for Danial.

It was announced that the midnight hour was approaching and everyone raised their goblet as they counted down the seconds, finally cheering and toasting as the clock hit twelve.

After this, the celebrations quietened down rapidly and the guests began to leave in dribs and drabs, each bidding farewell to Mother Christmas as they did. Danial felt sad that this wonderful festival was coming to an end.

The dormice and hedgehogs returned to their beds; Albi was yawning loudly as he did so, stuffed to the gunnels just as Hazel had predicted. All were now ready for sleep.

The last to leave was John Barleycorn, who was dancing and having fun until the bitter end. But the night had now waned and so reluctantly he disappeared into the stag head oak, waving to Danial with one hand as he went, a goblet still in the other.

Cervanae looked fondly at Danial and said softly, "We must go." The young boy looked disappointed, but knew the fun had come to an end.

"It is late, take my hand."

Danial halfheartedly obeyed and in the blink of an eye he was on top of the snowy roof of Frankly Hall. He looked around, astonished. How did they get here so quickly?

"Magic," Cervanae said, answering the question Danial had not yet even asked. She pointed ahead, telling him, "Yonder, there is a doorway. Follow the steps downwards and you will be safely back inside."

Danial hugged his friend tightly and with a beaming smile said, "Thank you so much for the present."

"Rest now," Cervanae smiled, "you have a big day tomorrow; so much must be decided."

"The meeting at the village hall?"

Cervanae nodded.

"We'll win," Danial cried, "I promise!

He waved a regretful farewell before disappearing through the small doorway.

Cervanae remained where she stood, pensive and concerned.

Will we win? Only time will tell, she thought.

Chapter Twenty-Seven

Lily screamed with excitement, she simply loved this time of year. She ran down the stairs towards the large Christmas tree, and inspected each enticing, shining present sitting at its base. Christmas itself was only a few days away and she was ready to erupt with unbridled joy.

Simon's mood did not reflect Lily's happiness. The weather outside had worsened, further affecting how he felt. It was snowing heavily across the country, which was the same temperature as the Arctic; it was the coldest lead-up to Christmas since records had begun. His stomach was in knots; the prospect of the meeting he had agreed to filled him with dread. It was not going to be easy – the villagers had already proven that.

He knew he would have to hold it together, clearly explaining the benefits of fracking and what good it could bring to the village. On a personal level, it would protect his family, bringing in the much-needed money to keep living in the large hall. His big problem was that he wasn't sure many of the villagers *could* be convinced; he would need to be perfect in his presentation.

The task in front of him was a hard one, especially now that even Ella was starting to have doubts after the way they'd all been treated by the local community. And, of course, Danial hated the idea too. Not only that, but all the nonsense about his 'friend' who lived in Frankly Woods was irritating to say the least. It was just a wildwood full of pests like rats and mice. And now even *Lily* was joining in with the fantasy, making up rubbish about flying sleighs. Simon wondered what kind of things his son had been telling Lily for her to make up such stories like this.

Lily's loud whoop snapped him back from his thoughts. Though he loved to see her happy, the excitement and noise wasn't helping one bit. Simon yearned for some quiet in order to fortify himself for the upcoming ordeal. He had not slept well of late; the nerves in his stomach did somersaults and awful thoughts spun round and round his head whenever he lay down in bed.

It's the most wonderful time of the year... at least that's how the song goes, Simon thought. Well, today's meeting at the village hall would prove whether that was true or not – *it's sink or swim time.*

***

Simon's anxiety did not ease one bit on his arrival at the village hall. Mr Carney and Mr Wyatt had picked him up and their sleek, black car drawing up outside village hall had not gone down well at all.

They entered the all to the sound of loud boos; the villagers were as unfriendly as they could be. Simon was glad Ella had stayed home with the children; this hostile a reception would have made her cancel the fracking idea immediately.

Even when seated, the frosty welcome didn't change, the boos in fact growing louder – and amongst this and the hissing, there were even hostile shouts.

Simon struggled to make his speech, but it was clear that the villagers were in no mood to compromise. With every word spoken, the negativity increased; so much so that the two men from Shale Oil quickly stepped in.

"Do you not understand the advantages that fracking will bring to your village?" Steve Wyatt cried with exasperation. "You will *all* benefit!"

"There are *no* benefits to be had!" Flynn Davies countered. "All I foresee is pollution, contaminated water, earthquakes...and what about my animals?"

"Exactly! A huge well bored deep into the ground isn't going to help them or us," Stan Abbott added passionately.

A chorus of agreement greeted his words.

"You're spreading make-believe horror stories though," Wyatt shouted above the growing racket. "You're worrying about things that won't happen."

It was no good though; the crowd was angry. Henry Carney stood up and raised his hands in an attempt to placate the villagers. It took a while, but the shouting did calm down into more of a murmur. He then spoke calmly and confidently.

"Please, we all need to calm down before a riot breaks out. What my colleague Mr Wyatt is trying to explain is that you will all benefit from the Shale Wealth Fund as soon as fracking goes ahead."

"Your attempts at bribery won't work on us," Veronica chided, "money isn't everything, you know."

Steve Wyatt muttered under his breath, "How could anyone think that?"

But Carney continued coolly.

"There is no *bribe*. The Shale Wealth Fund was set up some years ago to help the economy of any area selected for fracking. Ten per cent of all proceeds from a fracking site will be funnelled into local councils and community trusts."

"Hah! *Now* we know why the council is so keen for fracking to go ahead," Stanley Abbott said, shaking his head in disgust, "it's to line their own pockets!"

The crowd nodded and muttered in agreement, but Carney continued in the same calm manner.

"Please, *please,* let me finish," he begged. "Listen, the British government is talking about monies made from a well site going straight into *individual households* affected by it. It'll not just be councils and trusts, but you will *all* prosper from this."

"Fine, but at what *cost?*" Mrs Briggs cried. "As we keep saying, we don't care about the money, Mr Carney, we care about our *lives*. You can't replace the hundreds of years of history and peace our community has experienced with *money*."

Then it happened.

"Speak for yourself," Peter Egan said; a short silence followed as angry faces glared at him.

Wyatt smiled at the breakaway villager. His hope now grew; their plan was working. They just had to convince a few more and that would be all the disagreement they would need. *Divide and conquer,* so the saying goes.

"For pity's sake, it's just a load of old trees," Egan pleaded to his fellow villagers. "With the money they say they'll give us, we could plant a whole new forest when they've drained all the gas. And just think of what else the village could gain?"

Mrs Briggs shook her head. "No, that's not right. You just don't understand the importance of *history*."

"I understand this could be a missed opportunity," said Wyatt.

Mrs Briggs sighed deeply. "Frankly Woods is mentioned in the Domesday Book. You're talking about wiping out a thousand years of history for greed, for profit. I say *no!* We will fight this until the bitter end."

Wyatt looked at her blankly; he had no idea what a Domesday Book was. Carney held one hand up in deference to Mrs Briggs's point.

"I take your point about history," he said, "and I know history is important, but... isn't our *environment* even more important than that? Think of your children, and your grandchildren. They need to grow up in a world that is thriving, not one that is dying because of companies extracting fossil fuels in the old, dirty, damaging way."

"But fracking will *ruin* our village," Veronica exclaimed, "it'll wreck the local environment!"

"No, You're wrong," Carney said firmly, shaking his head. "Fracking is more environmentally friendly than other extraction methods. That's surely a good thing? Now, let me address your concerns one-by-one. You talk of pollution, water shortages, methane, transport noise and earthquakes, so let's start with—"

"Isn't pollution alone enough?" Flynn Davies barked.

"It is… and it isn't," the Texan replied. "Look, many governments have developed regulations that assess fracking risks. In the UK alone, the regulatory framework states that the risks are manageable when carried out under proper guidelines. The rules say that any oil or gas company has to minimize pollution as a condition of their license."

The words sounded reassuring, and as the crowd digested them there was a murmur of quiet discontent. Carney took the lull as an invitation to continue.

"Now, you also mentioned 'contaminated water'. The risks here are minimal. Once water has been used for the fracking process, it becomes *waste* water. This gets treated and if it's not removed from a site immediately, we place it in a *wastewater well* to be reused at a future fracking site. Your mains water supply will be completely separate from any such toxic waste."

The murmur began to grow louder, as if questions or concerns were about to be shouted out. Henry Carney was on a roll however, and decided to continue before the chaos erupted again.

"Next, let me address the methane gas issue. It *is* true that methane release can be a problem in older wells. But the Frankly well will be a new one, so the dangers will be practically nonexistent. The government is as we speak developing regulations to access and manage any environmental or health risks. We wouldn't be permitted to frack unless it was safe, and stringent rules and regulations were in place."

The crowds anger was now clearly growing.

"Finally, why don't we talk about the danger of earthquakes, which—"

It felt like there was an earthquake in the village hall. Or, perhaps, a volcano. The eruption of discontent hit Carney like a giant wave crashing hard on the shore. He raised his voice and attempted to continue over the racket.

"—which are scare stories designed to frighten you like a Halloween monster."

"The benefits from fracking *far* outweigh the risks," Wyatt stated, once again joined the fray. "Not only is fracking great for the economy, but it's also good for the environment too. Shale gas is a cleaner source of energy, CO_2 emissions can be reduced by up to fifty per cent compared to older methods. It's the next phase of fossil fuel energy, fit for future generations."

"If fracking is so wonderful," Shirley Abbott shouted, "why don't you frack where *you* live?"

Raucous laughter followed her words.

"You're just trying to put a positive spin on a complete negative," Veronica Michaels added, joining in with the fight. "We're not blind, we're not uneducated, we've done our research. A deep well can use up to fifty thousand gallons of water for a single fracture. It *would* affect our water supply, our rivers, our lakes!" She looked directly at Carney and continued, "You talk of waste water. When you frack, this can come back up, it can escape into the local environment. What happens then?"

"We have *procedures!*" the Texan stressed. "We have clean-up processes that meet the regulations. We—"

"You're talking about drilling a vertical well and forcing a what equates to a tsunami down it. This causes stress to the surrounding rocks. Then, when removing the waste water, those vertical walls can collapse. Any such stress on the underground rock can lead to an earthquake!"

The villagers roared their discontent.

Veronica continued, the bit between her teeth, "Don't even get me started on the methane emissions, which would pollute the very air that our children breathe!"

Wyatt tried to hide his surprise at Veronica's knowledge of the subject. Maybe these people were not as dumb as he'd originally thought.

Now Flynn made a contribution. "There's also the farmland to consider. All those toxic chemicals seeping into the soil? Awful. And my sheep need peace, particularly in the springtime as stress can cause them to lose their lambs. But the peace we have always enjoyed here would be shattered by all the noise the additional transport needed would create. Unless, that is, you intend to ship things in and out on Father Christmas's sleigh?"

A howl of laughter filled the hall.

Mrs Briggs added her dissent. "We don't want trucks and diggers trundling right past our front doors at all hours of the day and night."

Veronica was pleased with the meeting's progress. She was proud that others had listened to her arguments and learned from them. She had been worried that she would be alone in the fight, that people would be tempted by greed... but instead was pleasantly surprised at the strength of the support for her view. Yes, Peter Egan was an exception, but she could deal with him later.

For the first time in quite a while, Simon spoke up.

"Do any of you actually think I would do something that would put my own family at risk? Surely you can see that I would never undertake anything that could harm them!"

"But you're prepared to harm *our* families, aren't you?" Veronica shouted.

Simon shook his head. "Fracking is the future. It's a more environmentally friendly way to power the country, and it would end our reliance on dangerous states such as Russia. We will all reap the rewards, if only you would give it a chance!"

"Answer me this question then," Veronica said with confidence. "If fracking is so safe, if it's so wonderful... then why have France, Germany and Scotland *completely banned it?*"

In honesty, Simon did not have a clue. He racked his brains for an answer, but before anything came to him, the door of the village hall flung open.

It was Danial.

All eyes in the village hall turned towards him as silence fell; this was an interesting development.

For a moment he was too nervous to say anything. Then, suddenly, he thought of the incredible festival he'd attended and found his voice.

"Dad, stop!" he shouted.

"Danial... what on earth?" Simon looked behind him, expecting to see Ella and Lily – but they were not there.

"Dad, you can't agree to the fracking. Don't do it!"

"Go home," demanded Simon. "We'll talk about this later."

"No!" Danial said, standing firm.

Astonished gasps followed, then Mrs Briggs said what everyone was thinking.

"See, even your *son* doesn't want you to go ahead!"

Simon's voice became angrier. "Does your mother know that you are here?"

The boy shook his head.

If steam could have spouted out of his father's ears, it would have. Simon frantically texted Ella.

"Danial, you will sit at the back and not say another word."

Danial knew that his father was ready to erupt, and he could get in a huge amount of trouble for this. But it was far too important... and he couldn't back out now.

"You can't destroy Frankly Woods Dad, because they're *magical!*"

The villagers were completely silent, but one laugh could be clearly heard. Steve Wyatt chuckled again, shaking his head in disbelief.

"This is ridiculous. Magic? Please. Mr Harper, this meeting is solely to inform the villagers of the plans you have told me you agree to. I don't wish to spend any more time in this godforsaken place. Control your awful son and tell these people you've made your decision.

The crowd erupted into shouts and boos.

Awful son.

Simon may well have been upset at Danial. But no-one had the right to talk about his child like that. He looked straight at Danial, who he could tell was on the verge of crying. Could what his son said really be true? Or even possible?

"Please Dad, I can show you," Danial pleaded loudly.

Simon shouted back over the din. "Show me? What?"

"Come with me to the woods, I'll prove it!"

"Oh, this is insanity!" Wyatt snapped. "You're talking nonsense boy, you're a disgrace to your family interrupting like this. If you were my son, I'm telling you now that you'd find out how to behave the hard way!"

The scraping of Simon's chair on the floor as he slowly stood up caused the din from the crowd to cease almost instantly.

"Luckily Mr Watt, he is *not* your son – he's mine. Danial, I hope this is no joke. Now show me."

A huge smile spread across Danial's face. He turned back through the doorway, beckoning his father, who ran to catch up with him.

Steve Wyatt's irate voice filled the air.

"This is madness; he's just seeking attention. Punish the child!"

Simon froze.

He turned back around to face the Americans.

"I think it's time for me to listen to my son. I'm going for a walk."

Without another word, he left the hall.

Chapter Twenty-Eight

Veronica Michaels, Mrs Briggs, Flynn Davies and all the other villagers stood up from their seats and bundled out of the hall.

Only the two Americans were left; they looked at each other, shrugged, then also jumped up out of their seats to follow the group.

Danial had taken his father's hand, and was leading him as quickly as he could down a frosty Ley Lane. From there, the two made their way to the edge of the woods, villagers and Americans following behind them.

"This way, Dad!" Danial said as he pulled his father deeper and deeper into the mass of snowy trees, the strange group of stragglers doing their best to keep up too.

"Here Dad, look!"

They reached the stag-head oak, the signpost to the previous day's midwinter feast. Excitement grew in Danial's stomach as he trod the now-familiar route, bringing them out to the clearing beyond.

"What's happened here?" Simon shouted, aghast.

He pushed past his son to examine the charred remains of the previous night's bonfire. He kicked the pile of cinders and ash, which was already beginning to vanish beneath the fresh dusting of white.

Wyatt caught up, panting heavily.

"Look! The villagers have destroyed your land – it's a protest to stop the fracking!"

"How *dare* you!" Veronica Michaels – at the front of the group of villagers – cried. "Our wish is to *protect* this land, not *destroy* it. Destroying nature is what *you* do!"

The whole fracking argument – this time with even more insults – erupted again between the American and the villagers.

"ENOUGH!"

Simon's roar completely filled the clearing, bringing the squabble to an abrupt end.

His eyes fixed on Danial.

"Son, tell me what happened here?"

"It was the Yule festival."

"The what?" Simon replied, looking at him blankly.

"It was the midwinter festival where we celebrated the shortest night of the year." He beamed a big smile.

"You caused this damage?" Simon asked with disbelief.

Danial shook his head. "No, Dad. It was Cervanae's feast day! What happened was that the Spirits of the Forest, the Steed of the Fairies and the Spriggan—"

"My God, he's bonkers!" howled Steve Wyatt. "Who next, Santa Claus?"

Simon's anger returned with a vengeance.

"We are going home, *now!*" he declared, grabbing Danial's hand, but the boy snatched it away.

"Dad, you *have* to believe me!"

"You told me that there were people living in the woods. You promised to show me that they were 'magical', as you said. And you bring me to see this? The remains of a fire? Haven't I taught you how dangerous something like this can be? I'm very, very disappointed in you, Danial."

"Magic is *real,* Dad!"

Steve Wyatt sniggered, his eyebrows raised so high that they almost fell off the top of his head.

"All that we've found here is that your son has caused serious damage... and may I suggest that he is too young to act alone?"

Simon's eyes narrowed, and he scanned the assembled villagers accusingly; they huffed indignantly at the suggestion that they'd had anything to do with the sight in front of them.

Wyatt grinned; he felt that he had made his point well, and that Simon was now leaning back to his way of seeing the world.

"I can't take any more of this nonsense. It's cold and I'm losing the feeling in my feet. Let's get back to the warmth and get the paperwork signed."

Danial looked around at the villagers, who held his gaze with pity.

Veronica Michaels shook her head sadly. "I don't think there's anything more to see here."

"Finally, we agree on something!" said Steve Wyatt, rubbing warmth into his frozen fingers. "Let's go."

He smirked, turned around, and began to tread back through the icy thicket. Carney, who had been the last to catch up with Simon and Danial, joined him.

"Cervanae, please show yourself," Danial pleaded.

He looked around, eyes searching in vain for any sign of his friend, or the celebrations that had taken place. But the trees were now devoid of their decorations, the tables had disappeared and the talking animals must have been all tucked up in their beds. There wasn't even a single greenie in sight.

Gloom enveloped Danial.

But then he suddenly remembered.

The verse!

"Of bird, of horse, of Ox, of deer,
I call for Cervanae to appear here.
Be quick, be swift, come my way,
I need your help this very day."

He waited expectantly; he knew Cervanae's imminent appearance would prove to his father that everything he said had been true.

But nothing happened.

Danial tried again.

"Of bird, of horse, of Ox, of deer,
I call for Cervanae to appear here.
Be quick, be swift, come my way,
I need your help this very day."

Still nothing.

He repeated the verse over and over again, but only silence filled the frozen air.

Danial had been brave, he'd remained strong... but now the first tear rolled down his cheek as a deep despondency filled his entire being.

Where *was* she?

"Dad, please just take me home," he sobbed.

All Simon could think about was what had caused his son to be like this. Stories, make-believe, imaginary friends... but now dangerous behaviour - making a bonfire? The child obviously needed help. Perhaps they could speak to a doctor...

Mrs Briggs then spoke to Danial in a kind tone.

"They only appear to those who accept them as real."

Danial looked up at her, shocked.

The old woman stared into the woodland darkness as if waiting for something, announcing, "There are too many disbelievers here."

Veronica Michaels looked at Mrs Briggs quizzically and asked, "What do you mean, *disbelievers?*"

"All this talk of money, oil, drilling, fracking... all material things, technology, modern-day stuff. But what about nature? Who here hasn't taken a walk in Frankly Woods and marvelled at the sights, the sounds, the smells... the *magic* of nature?"

Danial was staring at her. *The magic of nature.* Did she *know?*

The villagers were completely silent, taking in Mrs Briggs's words. Yes, it was true that Frankly Woods felt like a 'magical' place, but that was just a saying, wasn't it? Magic wasn't *real,* surely?

Chapter Twenty-Nine

It had been silent for around thirty seconds, each person contemplating the situation. Simon was about to take Danial's hand and lead him home when a strange humming sound began.

In front of him, a small light suddenly appeared; it seemed to be the source of the noise. The light began to grow larger, its brightness almost blinding Simon, Danial, the Americans and the villagers who had all been staring at it.

Then, without warning, there was a large CRACK and the light disappeared. People rubbed their eyes as they adjusted back to normal from the intensity of the orb.

Simon's mouth dropped open at the sight in front of him. The shock sent a rush of adrenalin through his body, and every instinct told him to run. But regardless of what his logical brain was telling him to do, his body would not obey. He stood there transfixed, mouth agape.

The snowy clearing had exploded into life.

Holly, Ivy, and Mistletoe draped snowy branches overhead, while lanterns hung from trees, below which gifts sparkled beneath bare branches like the brightest jewels. Smells and noise and colour and movement overwhelmed every single one of his senses.

Then, what looked like tiny bulbs of light seemed to descend from nowhere, darting all around the clearing.

Simon blinked his eyes, and in that fraction of a second, a young girl appeared, standing in the centre of the burnt remains, her long white cloak flowing down to the ground. All around her were animals of every type, some even that Simon didn't recognise.

"Welcome, Simon, father of Danial," said the girl, smiling.

"CERVANAE!" Danial shouted, running past his father towards her, "I *knew* you'd come!" He cried tears of joy as he threw his arms tightly around his friend.

Besides them stood Aurochs and Tarpan, a mass of Robin Redbreasts still chittering on the mighty steed's back.

"I would never abandon you!" She said, hugging him to her, white cape floating on the icy breeze "It took all my power, but this is the strength of our friendship."

Simon was not the only one astonished by what he saw. Behind him, the villagers gasped as they took in the wondrous scene. Some had begun to return to the village, but had turned back towards the clearing on seeing the flash of light.

Steve Wyatt gasped as the tiny lights flew towards him, buzzing around his face like bees to a honeypot. As they came close, he realised they were fireflies. A chorus of tiny voices berated him as Oberon landed on top of his nose, glaring with menace.

"Do not mess with the Greencoats!"

A growling hiss that seemed to come from near to the treeline caught Wyatt's attention.

"You poisonous *oik!*"

He scanned around himself with fearful eyes.

"Who said that?"

"I!" shouted the Spriggan as it appeared suddenly beside him.

The sapling stepped towards the oilman, growing ever bigger as it did, morphing from a shrivelled hag into a wizened old man. With a wave of its branch, it summoned a swarm of hornets and sent them flying in Wyatt's direction.

The American turned and fled back through the trees yelling at the top of his lungs, all the while chased by the angry swarm. The tiny greenies followed the throng, their berating voices floating back to the clearing on the icy air.

Cervanae laughed.

"One should not make an enemy of the Spriggan, nor the fairy-folk!"

"Fairies?" Simon croaked, able to speak only now for the first time.

"You doubt your own eyes, Simon, father of Danial?" Cervanae questioned, looking at him. "What is it that you do not believe?"

Simon stammered, "Y— You're not supposed to exist!"

Cervanae gestured around herself to the multitude of animals. "Then all of us are just in your imagination, are we?"

Simon turned to looked at the villagers and Carney, who were also dumbstruck by the magical scene.

"I told you, Dad!" Danial cried. "Frankly Woods are *special!*"

Mrs Briggs clapped her hands to her mouth almost in prayer. A cry of delight left her lips, tears running down her cheeks.

Cervanae bowed deeply to her.

"Welcome back, Anna, daughter of Michael. It has been an age."

"Too many years to count," the old woman smiled.

Cervanae nodded.

"The world has changed greatly since we last met. Then it was a country at war; a time we hope never to be repeated."

"That it was; oh yes," Mrs Briggs agreed. "You look well, Mother Christmas, exactly how I remember you - you haven't changed one jot."

"The earth grows older, but nature survives; it always stays the same."

The villagers' mouths dropped open, every single one questioning the reality of the scene they were watching intensely.

Danial looked from Cervanae to Mrs Briggs and then back again. Clearly he was not the only one to have met Cervanae.

"So you know each other?"

"I was much younger then, Master Danial; I was a child like you are now," Mrs Briggs answered. "It was a whole country in crisis, not just Frankly Woods."

"Man's need to destroy." Cervanae added sagely.

"*Some* destroy," Mrs Briggs shook her head, "but others do save."

"Like you!" Cervanae said, smiling with kindness.

"I am the Lady of the Forest, protector of this ancient land, the goddess of old, the Earth Mother. Be proud of your achievements, Anna. You *did* help fight for nature."

Mrs Briggs burst into a sob at the words of her long-lost friend, remembering her youth with a clarity she hadn't been able to for a long, long time. She buried her head on the shoulder of the closest person to her, which happened to be Henry Carney's. For a moment he didn't know what to do, but then gently patted the crying woman.

Cervanae took Mrs Briggs's hand and whispered a while into her ear. Soon, the tears stopped and broad smile spread across her face.

"You are right, Mother Christmas," she said. "We cannot go back, however much we want to. The past *has* passed. So we must look forward, living our lives to the best of our ability."

Cervanae nodded, her doe eyes falling onto Simon once more.

"You must not allow the fracking to take place, father of Danial. This magical land, this ancient woodland, cannot be destroyed."

"But I really don't have a choice." Simon pleaded, looking perturbed. "It's the only way I can protect the estate, my wife and my children."

"What's going on?" said a voice.

It was Ella, who had reached the clearing with Lily.

"I got to the village hall to find nobody there, until Mr Wyatt ran past me screaming. He was being chased down the road by what looked like a swarm of giant bees and a horde of flying lights! There were two boys hiding inside the hall - Nathan and Freddy Davies - who told me where you had all gone too. But no matter how much I tried to persuade them, they wouldn't come into the woods with me. So I used the torch on my mobile to follow your footsteps in the snow. Those boys were clearly frightened of something, fearful of *something*."

"They're scared of John Barleycorn," Danial smirked.

It was only now that Ella really took in the scene that greeted her. The clearing was almost glowing, pulsating like a heartbeat; Cervanae standing with Danial, her white cape shimmering in as if covered by diamonds; the strange assembled creatures and the crowd of villagers. For some reason, it reminded Ella of a snow globe.

"Who's John Barleycorn?" Flynn Davies spat. "If he's done anything to my children, then—"

"Me!" cried the wild man of the woods as he sprang from the stag-head oak like a jack-in-the-box.

"Arrgh!" cried Flynn Davies, falling backwards onto the snow as John jumped from tree to tree joyfully, then landed right on his chest.

"Your sons are *bullies,"* the wild man scolded hotly, squeezing Flynn's nose and making a 'parp' sound. Then as quickly as he'd appeared, he bounced right back towards the oak and disappeared into the large knot on its trunk.

For a moment Flynn lay there winded, utterly terrified by what had just happened to him.

Then he found his feet.

Like his sons he ran as fast as his legs would carry him. Others moved to follow, terror etched on their faces... but Cervanae's words stopped them.

"Do not fear, the 'wild' man is wild in name only; you are all safe."

The soothing assurance appeared to calm those gathered.

"Come, meet my mum," Danial said to Cervanae, taking his friend's hand. Cervanae smiled as she was led towards the new arrival.

"Good evening, Ella, mother of Danial and Lily."

Like Simon, Ella found it hard to believe what she was seeing. She couldn't understand where the glow that surrounded this young girl was coming from. She was brought back to reality when Lily ran towards Cervanae and hugged her.

"This is Danial's friend, Mummy."

Cervanae beamed. Lily looked up at her, eyes wide.

"Can we go on another sleigh ride?"

"A *sleigh ride?*" Ella gasped, remembering Lily's words. Even though her practical head could still not quite believe everything her children had said to her about healed bones and magical sleigh rides, she realised she could not doubt her own eyes.

Danial was *not* a liar; his friend was real and was standing right before her.

Cervanae chuckled, "Not today, sweet one. This day we have more pressing matters to discuss."

Normally, a refusal like this would be met by screams, tears or tantrums. Yet today, Lily was as good as gold.

Simon and Ella looked at each other gobsmacked.

"Now, where were we?" Cervanae said, walking back to join Tarpan and Aurochs. "Oh yes; it's *not* the only way. There are others, Simon, father of Danial."

Simon looked at her expectantly.

"You could farm the land."

Simon shook his head. "Farming? I'd have no idea where to start or what to do; I'm a city boy!"

"We'll help you!" Mrs Briggs cried.

"But farming alone isn't going to save the estate," Simon exclaimed.

"You could also use Frankly Hall," Cervanae said.

Simon looked at her blankly.

Mrs Briggs nodded, clapping her hands.

"Yes, yes! You have a beautiful house, Mr Harper. You could try hosting different events... like weddings! Oh yes, with a bit of spit and polish, I'm sure that *any* bride would be proud to be married at the Hall!"

Simon grew thoughtful, the ideas starting to whirr rapidly through his brain.

"There's also ghost hunts, aren't there?" Veronica Michaels piped up, joining the discussion. "People pay a fortune these days to be scared witless. And us villagers could help."

"We *all* would," Mrs Briggs nodded. "*Anything* to stop the woods and our homes from being destroyed."

"There are so many options, Mr Harper," agreed Doctor White. "Don't ruin this beautiful place for profit alone."

"Please! Mum, Dad?" Danial pleaded, the snow growing heavier around them.

His cry stirred Ella, who had been half-listening in a dreamlike state. Like Simon, ideas for the hall bombarded her brain.

Before they could answer the fireflies returned, buzzing around the astonished group, who quickly realized that they were beautiful, tiny winged fairies. Joy and laughter spread over the assembled crowd.

Oberon flew over to Henry Carney and landed on top of his nose. The Texan was astonished as he was admonished by the tiny greenie, whose robes floated delicately on the icy air.

Simon and Ella looked at the other, eyes falling back onto the beauty of the magical scene. Could they *really* try something different to save the hall?

For what felt an age to the villagers, the two huddled together in deep discussion, all the while snow whipping around them. Simon asked Mr Carney to come over and the three spent even more time in quiet discussion.

Danial felt like he was in his bedroom again, with every second feeling like a minute was ticking by. He shifted impatiently from foot to foot.

Finally, Simon turned to face everyone.

"I think we're going to go ahead—"

A wail of disappointment filled the group. Faces fell, gloom and tears etched on each one.

"—with the hosting of many different events!"

It took a moment for everyone to take in the words.

Then, a loud cry of excitement exploded.

The cry became a cheerful dance, couples hugging each other, animals chirping and carousing in a chorus of gleeful noise, the whole wood coming to life.

"Really?" Danial said as he threw himself at his parents, hugging them tightly.

Lily joined them and a group hug ensued. Simon ruffled his son's head and spoke.

"What right do we have to destroy what has been here since time began? This land must be protected for future generations; the fracking must be stopped." His gaze held Cervanae's. "Not just for us but for nature itself."

Cervanae smiled.

"Thank you, Simon, father of Danial."

Henry Carney then coughed and all eyes fell upon him. He sighed, the said, "After what I've seen here, if Mr and Mrs Harper had not made the right decision, then I would have anyway. The oil company will get an email tomorrow stating it is a most unsuitable place for a test well. You have my word, there will be no fracking here."

Joyous cheers filled the air as Carney continued.

"I can't destroy such a wondrous place. I have lived a long time and before today I honestly thought I'd seen everything. How wrong I was."

"What about Mr Wyatt?" Ella enquired, looking worried.

"Don't you worry about him. If Steve Wyatt opens his mouth about any of this, he'll be looking for new employment."

Oberon and Mab bowed to the Texan, who removed his hat and bobbed his head in response.

"Thank you Henry," Simon said, shaking his hand vigorously.

Cervanae turned to Tarpan, reaching for something on top of his back. It was a small piece of burnt wood that she handed to Danial.

"This is special. Guard it well until next midwinter. I think you know where it should be placed.

Danial's brow furrowed; for a moment he really didn't know.

Then it hit him.

The glass container in the hidden priest hole! There had been a small piece of burnt wood in it. That must have been last year's yule log that was used to light this one!

Danial sighed happily.

As it goes, his secret tunnel had turned out not to be so boring after all.

THE END

Printed in Dunstable, United Kingdom